# Alien Incursion

## The Tactical Advantage Series – Book Two

Sean Patrick Posey

This is an original publication of Sean Patrick Posey.



Text design by Sean Patrick Posey

3D Battle Carrier design by Sean Patrick Posey

3D Battle Carrier model by Sean Patrick Posey

Front cover design by Sean Patrick Posey

Front cover artwork by Sean Patrick Posey



FIRST EDITION: January 2019

SECOND EDITION: December 2019

Posey, Sean Patrick

Alien Incursion/Sean Patrick Posey - Second Edition

Science Fiction – Fiction

You can see other titles I have available on my website:

**seanpatrickposey.com**

## ACKNOWLEDGEMENTS

For Nicole, my sweet, beautiful, loving wife who encouraged me to write this book, and for my sweet beautiful daughters Alyssa and Sarah for whom I would do anything. I love you all.

# TABLE OF CONTENTS

Prologue....05
Chapter 1 – Forced Flight....06
Chapter 2 – Surprise Attack....17
Chapter 3 – Tragedy....41
Chapter 4 – Back To Trynx 3....72
Chapter 5 – Another Loss....81
Chapter 6 – Special Forces....104
Chapter 7 – Betrayal And Revenge....123
Chapter 8 – Starting Over....149
Chapter 9 – No More Time....179
Chapter 10 – The Plan....191
Chapter 11 – Goodbye Trynx 3....205
Epilogue....223
Glossary....224

# PROLOGUE

After the recent Sulari incident, Earth's World Council decided they must fully secure the planet Trynx 3 to prevent anyone from getting their hands on even a small piece of its most valuable commodity.

Trynx 3 is the only known source of a very special and potentially very dangerous ore. An ore with temporal properties that could be (and recently was) used to power a time machine. In the wrong hands, a time machine could be the most dangerous weapon ever built.

Until such time that a method for safely eliminating this ore is found, the World Council ordered the Earth Defense Force (EDF) to establish a military presence at Trynx 3 in the form of a battle group, a military space station and a web of defense satellites.

In addition, a civilian contractor was hired to design and implement a multi-layered planetary monitoring system to help prevent any unauthorized landings or takeoffs.

# CHAPTER 1 – FORCED FLIGHT

It's true what they say, you shouldn't pass judgment on people you don't know because you have no idea what is going on in their lives or what is motivating them to do what they are doing.

John Tisdale is the lead systems design engineer for the company that was awarded the contract to implement a multi-layered planetary monitoring system on Trynx 3. John arrived on Trynx 3 six months ago and he is almost ready to bring the monitoring system online. Every night since he arrived, John could be found working in his office in the ore mine's high security outpost until well after midnight.

John has never done anything illegal in his life, but that is about to change. Tonight, John is not in his office working, tonight he is sneaking into the outpost's inner compound dressed in black, sporting a tactical helmet with night vision and a pulse rifle he "borrowed" from a guard.

John can hear and feel his heart pounding in his ears. His adrenaline level has spiked, causing the "everything is happening in slow motion" effect. He takes several deep breaths, attempting to calm his nerves.

Not wanting to hurt anyone, he sets the pulse rifle to stun then brings it up so he can look through the sights as he moves. He crouches low and makes his way across the compound, trying to be as quiet as possible, staying in the shadows and hiding behind various crates, barrels, and parked vehicles. John does his best to mimic what he has seen in the movies when a tactical team is trying to sneak in undetected, pausing at every object to listen and turning to "check his six" every twenty-five feet.

Finally, after what seems like an eternity, John reaches a trio of mining trucks, parked in a line, twenty yards from his objective, the outpost armory. He makes his way in between the two trucks that are closest to the armory and kneels down beside the front tires to look underneath. There it is, the entrance to the armory and the two armed guards standing right in front of it.

"Shit," John whispers.

He checks his watch and sees there is sixty seconds left on the timer he set. Sixty seconds until the program he wrote takes down all the force fields, security sensors and cameras throughout the outpost.

John carefully crawls under the closest mining truck and takes aim through the scope on the pulse rifle. He is shaking so badly he can't keep his sights on target. He wipes the sweat off his brow and away from his eyes. Once again, he hears his heart pounding in his ears. He closes his eyes and takes several deep breaths, attempting to calm his nerves. It seems to help, hopefully enough.

He wipes the sweat away from his eyes again and takes aim. The timer on his watch reaches zero and beeps. He takes a deep breath, breathes out slowly and squeezes the trigger, stunning the first guard. Before the second guard can react, John puts the cross hairs on him and pulls the trigger again.

With both guards down, he waits, hoping and praying that nobody saw or heard the discharges from the pulse rifle, or saw the guards fall. He waits for twenty seconds. No alarms, nobody comes running to see what happened to the guards. All clear.

John crawls out from under the truck and attempts to get to his feet. He gets dizzy, weak at the knees and he feels like he's going to be sick. He sits down on the step of the truck for a few seconds until the dizziness and the urge to throw up goes away.

"Got to get moving. Got to get in, find what I'm looking for and get out before someone sees that the guards are missing."

He gets to his feet, peeks around the front of the truck and, upon seeing the coast is clear, sprints the twenty yards to the armory entrance.

Crouching in the shadow of the entrance alcove, sweat pouring out from under his helmet, he peers around the compound to see if anyone saw him running. He doesn't see anyone in the compound at all.

"Good, nobody saw me," he thinks to himself.

John looks up and sees, just above his head, mounted on the alcove wall, is a biometric hand scanner. His eyes shift from the hand scanner to the two unconscious guards then back to the scanner.

Cautiously he steps out, grabs one guard and drags him back into the shadow of the alcove, propping him up against the wall. When the first guard is stabilized, John grabs the second guard and drags him into the alcove. This time instead of leaning him against the wall, John pulls his right arm up and places his hand on the scanner.

A thick white line of light scans from the tips of the guard's fingers to the heel of his palm. The scanner then turns red, emits an error buzz and displays a message that says, "Unable To Identify, Please Ensure Proper Placement Of All Fingers On Scanner."

"Oh, come on already," he whispers.

John spreads the guard's fingers out and places his hand over the guard's hand to ensure proper contact. The white light scans the guard's hand again, this time the scanner turns green and displays a message that says, "Access Granted, Corporal Ramirez."

"Oh, thank God," he whispers.

The armory door unlocks with a loud metallic clang, startling John. The drive motor kicks in and swings the thick, metal door open. As soon as the door is open far enough, John drags Corporal Ramirez inside. He then runs back out and drags the other guard inside. Once inside he whacks the large red button to close the armory door again. The door closes and locks with another loud metallic clang.

There are no windows in the armory so John turns on all the lights so he can find what he is looking for quickly. No sense sneaking around in the dark when you don't have to.

At the other end of the armory John sees a chain link lock up. Instinct tells him that's where he will find what he is looking for. There are racks upon racks of weapons and explosives all throughout the high security armory building that are not locked up in a secondary secured area, so what would be? Something that the commanding officer didn't want anyone getting near, something very dangerous and potentially very valuable.

John sets his pulse rifle to its highest setting, aims at the lock on the gate and pulls the trigger. The lock, and everything within ten inches of it, disintegrates and the gate swings open. He walks in and finds several stacks of unmarked, wooden crates of various sizes. He grabs a crowbar from the workbench outside the lockup and pops the top off one of the medium sized crates. Inside he finds his prize, one hundred pounds of the Trynx 3 ore. John stares at this reddish-brown rock for a few seconds pondering how his life has taken a sharp turn because of it.

Snapping back to reality he realizes he needs to get the hell out of there, so he goes back to the workbench and grabs a hammer. He nails the crate shut again and carries it over to the armory door. He throws the crate on a small anti-gravity hand truck, turns off the lights and then whacks the big red button to open the door. The door unlocks with another loud metallic clang and swings open.

John sets his pulse rifle back to stun, whacks the big red button to close the door, and steps out of the armory pulling the hand truck behind him. The door closes and locks with yet another loud metallic clang. How nobody hears the huge metal door open or close is a mystery to John.

He waits for a few seconds in the alcove, to make sure the coast is clear, then turns to the right and heads behind the armory. There is a narrow stretch of ground between the back of the armory and the outpost perimeter wall that is never patrolled by guards, so John runs through it as fast as he can, pulling the hand truck behind him. When he reaches the end of the armory building, he stops and peers around the corner to check for patrolling guards.

John sees no one, so he drops to one knee to wait and catch his breath. He undoes the chin strap of his tactical helmet, takes it off, drops it on the ground, pulls a cloth out of his pocket and wipes the sweat off his face and forehead. He stuffs the cloth back in his pocket, puts his helmet back on, stands up and peeks around the corner. Again, John sees no one, so he sprints from the armory building over to a stack of crates, about thirty yards away.

Peering around the crates, John sees an aviation fuel truck, and beyond that he sees his target destination, a military troop transport sitting on the landing pad with the rear loading ramp open and ready to go.

"Just another sixty yards and I'm home free," he whispers.

With his adrenaline levels spiked, John sprints to the fuel truck, pauses to see if the coast is clear and continues on to the transport. When he reaches the rear ramp, he runs right up the ramp and into the cargo hold. As soon as he enters the cargo hold, the overhead lights turn on and John whacks the big red button on the wall to close the ramp. The hydraulics that open and close the ramp are not exactly quiet nor are they overly quick so John is praying that nobody hears or sees the ramp closing.

"Come on already," he says in a hushed tone.

The ramp closes with a fairly loud metallic clang which most definitely sounded a lot louder in John's head, and he thinks to himself, "Crap somebody must have heard that."

John hurries to secure the crate of ore for takeoff. He kills the power to the anti-gravity hand truck, and straps both it and the crate to the deck in the cargo hold.

John removes and drops his tactical helmet on the deck and runs to the front of the cargo hold. He climbs the ladder to the upper level of the transport and enters the cockpit. With his heart racing, he sits down in the pilot's seat which then slides forward moving him closer to the controls. Systems all around him illuminate and start up.

When John was sent to Trynx 3 he was put through a survival course which included emergency escape procedures. He was shown how to use the automated systems built in to the military transports to get off the planet if no military pilots were available.

Remembering his training, John says, “Computer, initiate emergency engine startup and takeoff.”

The computer answers in a female voice, “Acknowledged, initiating emergency engine startup and takeoff.”

The jet engines whine and spin up, getting louder and louder by the second. Through the cockpit windows John can see flood lights turning on throughout the compound and he can see armed military personnel running into the compound through various doors in the main complex.

It feels a hell of a lot longer to John, but after a mere thirty seconds the engines are up to speed, the throttles ram forward and the ship lifts off.

John looks out the cockpit windows and sees some of the soldiers dropping to one knee and aiming their pulse rifles at his transport as it rises.

John's eyes open wide and he yells, “OH SHIT! COMPUTER, SHIELDS UP, MAXIMUM POWER!”

“Acknowledged, shields up, maximum power.”

The soldiers on the ground fire their pulse rifles at the ascending transport, but with the shields at full power they have no effect at all.

When the transport clears two hundred feet, the engines change from vertical takeoff mode to flight mode. The transport starts to move forward, accelerating as the engine thrust cones pivot.

John needs to get off this planet, so he buckles his safety restraints and says, “Computer, initiate emergency climb, head for space.”

“Acknowledged, initiating emergency climb.”

The ship pulls up sharply, and the computer kicks the afterburners in. John feels very heavy as he is pushed back into his seat by the 4G climb.

Over the radio John hears the outpost air traffic controller alerting the patrolling fighters in the area of his unauthorized takeoff.

“Tomcats 270 and 287 this is Trynx Base. We have had an unauthorized takeoff. Transport 186 is climbing through angels 10, vector 275 degrees. Pursue and intercept.”

“Roger Trynx Base, Tomcats 270 and 287 moving to intercept.”

The pilot of Tomcat 270 switches his radio so that only his wingman can hear him and says, “Okay, let’s kick in the afterburners and go get him.”

“Roger that, kicking in the afterburners.”

Both pilots push their throttles wide open and are immediately pushed back in their seats from the acceleration. The tactical computers in the fighters show the transport about one hundred and ten miles away at about fifteen thousand feet and climbing. The top speed of an F-114 Tomcat is Mach 8.5 and the top speed of the transport is only Mach 2.0, so it won’t take long for the fighters to catch up to the transport.

John looks down at his tactical display and sees the two fighters approaching fast from astern.

“SHIT!”

In just under two minutes the fighters have caught up to him. They slow to match the transport’s speed and take up escort positions.

John looks out his side windows and sees a fighter off each wing. Sheer panic doesn’t even begin to describe what he is feeling.

“Attention Transport 186, this is Tomcat 270. You are instructed to return to base immediately, please acknowledge.”

John doesn’t answer.

“Attention Transport 186, this is Tomcat 270. You are instructed to land, return to base and land immediately, please acknowledge.”

Again, John doesn’t answer.

“Trynx Base, this is Tomcat 270. I can see the pilot looking at me so I know he can see and hear me, but there is no response from Transport 186. What are your instructions?”

“Tomcat 270 this is Trynx Base, take him out.”

“Roger Trynx Base.”

John looks to his left at Tomcat 270 and sees the pilot motioning downwards three times, pointing at the ground with his index finger.

“Transport 186, this is Tomcat 270. Last chance. Return to base and land immediately or we will shoot you down.”

The pilot rolls his plane ninety degrees to port so John can see the missiles on the belly of his fighter are ready to shoot, then he rolls it back.

John ignores his threat.

The pilot of Tomcat 270 switches his radio so that only his wingman can hear him and says, "Tomcat 287, pull back and trail at two kilometers."

"Roger that, pulling back to trail at two kilometers."

Tomcat 287 peels off and loops around to take up a follow position two kilometers behind the transport.

Tomcat 270 pulls back on the power to slow down and maneuvers directly behind John's transport at a distance of about a kilometer.

John's transport is quickly approaching the edge of the planet's atmosphere, and he is praying he's going to make it into space.

Wiping the sweat from his forehead, John yells, "COME ON, I DON'T WANT TO DIE!"

"Computer, bring the FTL drive online, plot a course for Meridian 3 and jump as soon as we clear the atmosphere."

"Acknowledged, bringing the FTL drive online. Course plotted. Thirty seconds to jump."

Just then the tactical computer beeps and says repeatedly, "Missile lock."

The pilot of Tomcat 270 pulls the trigger on his flight stick, a missile drops down a few feet below the belly of the Tomcat, the rocket engine ignites, and the missile screams off across the sky, closing rapidly on John's transport.

The tactical computer emits a solid high-pitched tone and says repeatedly, "Missile inbound."

John's sweaty hands are squeezing the arms of his seat as tight as he can, and he is pushing himself back into his seat.

He yells, "SHIT! COMPUTER, EVASIVE MANEUVERS! FIRE COUNTER-MEASURES!"

"Acknowledged, evasive maneuvers, firing counter-measures."

The computer rolls the transport over several times to port and pulls up even more. Flares and chaff fire from the launchers in the transport's belly.

John closes his eyes tight and yells, "AHHHHHHHHHHHH!"

John almost passes out from the high G maneuvers.

The counter-measures work, drawing the missile away from the transport and fooling it into detonating harmlessly. John hears the explosion and the transport shakes from the concussion.

John opens his eyes and yells, "SON OF A BITCH THAT WAS CLOSE!"

The sky in front of John's transport turns black and the stars come into view. John can also see four heavy cruisers from the orbiting fleet moving to intercept him. Those cruisers are getting bigger and bigger the closer they get.

"OH SHIT! COMPUTER, HOW LONG UNTIL WE JUMP?"

"FTL jump in ten seconds."

Once again, the tactical computer beeps and says repeatedly, "Missile lock."

The pilot of Tomcat 270 pulls the trigger on his flight stick, sending a second missile screaming off across the sky towards John's transport.

The tactical computer again emits a solid high-pitched tone and says repeatedly, "Missile inbound."

John watches the missile approaching for several seconds on the tactical display while yelling, "COME ON! COME ON! COME ON!"

When the missile is two seconds from impact the computer says, "Initiating FTL jump."

The transport accelerates away rapidly and disappears in a bright blue flash of light, leaving the missile behind to curve off harmlessly and fall back to Trynx 3.

“Trynx Base, this is Tomcat 270. Transport 186 has engaged his FTL drive and escaped. Transmitting sensor data and last known trajectory now.”

“Tomcat 270, this is Trynx Base. Acknowledged. Return to base.”

“Acknowledged Trynx Base. Tomcats 270 and 278 RTB.”

John slumps back in his chair, soaked in sweat, totally exhausted. His hands shaking from the adrenaline, his heart still pounding in his ears. It’s been one hell of a night.

# CHAPTER 2 – SURPRISE ATTACK

Solaris 5, a lush, beautiful world with many amazing natural wonders. A warm, tropical, resort planet covered in rain forests, deep blue oceans and thousands of miles of white sandy beaches. It's a popular destination for those who want to get away from it all, relax, lie on the beach, and soak up the sun.

Unfortunately, not everyone visiting Solaris 5 is there to relax. Captain Nathan Stone of Earth's Planetary Police and his crew are visiting Solaris 5 on police business.

They have received reports of an alien committing a whole list of crimes such as assaulting and robbing tourists, breaking and entering, theft, and destruction of private property. They arrived on Solaris 5 this morning and have been interviewing the victims.

The victims described the alien as being about seven feet tall, very muscular, with four arms, two legs, four dark, tear drop shaped eyes (two large and two small), a small bump with a small slit for a nose, pointed ears, a set of gills just below his ears, a small spiny fin on the top of his head and vibrant blue skin.

After getting this description Nathan and his team split up to see if they could find this alien. Nathan and his navigator, David Black form team one. Tactical officer, Aleena Norata and the communications officer, Desiree Arnoult form team two. Chief engineer, Hiro Nagata and pilot, James Bell form team three.

The three teams start at the large swimming pool at the center of the resort and work their way out, each team picking a different direction.

It doesn't take long for Nathan and Mr. Black to spot the tall, blue alien from across the courtyard. The alien was coming out of the front door of one of the guest bungalows carrying a sack over his shoulder. Nathan and Mr. Black assume the alien has broken into this bungalow and is now casually walking out with a sack full of valuables.

Nathan touches his earpiece to activate his radio and says, "We have eyes on the alien. He just entered the courtyard north of the swimming pool, in front of the second row of bungalows. All teams converge and approach with caution."

Ms. Norata answers, "On our way, Captain."

Mr. Bell answers, "Be right there, Captain."

The two teams turn and start running north as fast as they can, eager to catch up to Nathan and Mr. Black to back them up. As they run, they must weave through the resort's sidewalks and avoid crashing into the people walking on them.

Nathan and Mr. Black draw their side arms, set them to stun and approach the alien from behind. They weave through a small maze of sidewalks and trimmed hedges, trying to be as stealthy as possible, so the alien doesn't see them and run. It takes Nathan and Mr. Black a couple minutes to catch up to the alien. They approach him from behind with their weapons pointed at him. The alien seems oblivious to their presence.

When they get within ten feet of the alien, they stop and Nathan yells, "PLANETARY POLICE, STOP RIGHT THERE! PUT THE SACK DOWN, AND PUT ALL FOUR HANDS ON TOP OF YOUR HEAD!"

The alien stops walking, he pauses for about ten seconds and then slowly turns and looks over his shoulder at Nathan and Mr. Black with a cold, blank stare.

The hair on the back of Nathan's neck stands up and a cold shiver goes down his back. Experience tells Nathan this alien's not going to give up, he's going to run. Nathan feels that all too familiar feeling in the pit of his stomach. He feels his adrenaline start to flow, and he feels his heart rate increase.

The alien suddenly pivots, throws the sack of stolen property at their heads and then starts to run. The two police officers drop to one knee and fire at the alien as the sack flies over their heads. Both Nathan and Mr. Black hit the alien with about six blasts each, but it seems to have little effect on the large, muscular alien.

Nathan says, "Crap, that's not good. I guess we do this the hard way."

Nathan and Mr. Black look at each other, groan and then sprint off in pursuit of the large, blue alien.

Nathan touches his earpiece to activate his radio and yells, "WE'RE IN PURSUIT OF THE BLUE ALIEN! HE'S RUNNING NORTH THROUGH THE RESORT TOWARDS THE FOREST! OUR BLASTERS ON STUN HAD NO EFFECT ON HIM, REPEAT NO EFFECT!"

The blue alien has long, muscular legs and he can run really fast. Nathan and Mr. Black are not sure they can catch up to him. They see the alien enter a man-made path through the forest. The path has many twists and turns as it meanders its way through this beautiful forest of old growth. Incredibly tall trees with huge bases, very similar to the redwoods back on Earth, as far as the eye can see.

There are many people walking, jogging, and biking on this path and the alien doesn't care if he knocks people down in his attempt to flee from the police. People facing towards him see him coming and step off the path to get out of his way. Unfortunately, he has been crashing right through people that are facing away from him, knocking them flying.

Nathan and Mr. Black are yelling, "PLANETARY POLICE, OUT OF THE WAY!," as they run so they don't accidentally collide with anyone.

After about two hundred yards, the alien comes to an intersection on the path. The alien collides with a man riding a bicycle through the intersection on the adjacent path. The man and his bike get knocked over, and the alien takes a tumble. When the alien gets back up to run, he is limping. He has gashed open his right shin in the collision and it is bleeding profusely.

Nathan and Mr. Black begin to gain on the alien now. However, this will quickly be a moot point as they are running out of path. Up ahead Nathan and Mr. Black can see that this section of the path ends at a viewing area overlooking a cliff.

The two police officers are within twenty meters when the alien runs into the viewing area at the end of the path. The alien runs up to the railing at the cliff's edge to see if there's an escape route.

When Nathan and Mr. Black enter the viewing area they stop and point their weapons at the alien. They are both severely out of breath from the chase, so they stay put and take a minute to catch their breath. They watch the alien run around the viewing area looking for a way out, but there isn't one. The cliff is a sheer drop and the surrounding forest is too dense. The alien realizes the only way out is through the police officers.

Nathan says, "All right, there's no place for you to go. Give it up. Get down on your knees and put your hands on your head."

The alien just stands there and stares menacingly back at Nathan, panting, trying to catch his breath, trying to decide what to do.

Nathan says, "Last chance. Get down on your knees and put your hands on your head."

The alien looks up at the sky and lets out a long, loud roar. At the same time, he flicks his forearms and hands sharply towards the ground. As he does this, two inch long claws extend out from all twenty of his fingertips like switchblades.

Nathan says, "Well, I guess he's not going to give up."

Mr. Black answers, "I guess not."

The alien charges.

An adrenaline rush hits both men causing everything to seem like it is happening in slow motion. A little excitement and panic sets in, their breathing gets faster, their hearts start to pound, and their minds are racing, examining the situation and exploring their options. Without being fully cognizant of it, both men take their fingers off the trigger guards, place them on the trigger and begin firing. They each hit the alien at least a dozen times as he closes the distance between them. Just as before the stun blasts from their weapons have little effect on the alien, only causing a minor muscle contraction on impact.

When the alien is only a couple meters away, he jumps into the air and pulls all four of his arms back to strike.

Nathan and Mr. Black dive to the side, Nathan goes right, and Mr. Black goes left. As they fall, they twist to keep their weapons on target and they both flick the selection lever on their weapons to the kill setting.

As the alien passes over top of them, they both pull their triggers. With even more adrenaline running through their systems, everything seems to be moving even slower than before. Nathan and Mr. Black watch the intense blue balls of energy leave the barrels of their weapons as they begin their flight up towards their target. Shots that in reality take a split second to hit their target, feel like they take thirty seconds to both men.

Both blasts hit the alien in the upper torso. Nathan and Mr. Black watch as the energy is absorbed by the alien's body and the impact causes his skin to ripple. The alien's body and limbs tense and contract, his eyes close as he winces in pain and his mouth opens to emit a painful screech. The alien plows into the ground face first and slides for a few feet. He doesn't move after coming to a stop.

Nathan and Mr. Black get up off the ground, keeping their weapons trained on the alien. Mr. Black cautiously approaches the alien and checks for signs of life while Nathan covers him. He looks back at Nathan and shakes his head.

"He's dead."

Nathan touches his earpiece to activate his radio and says, "The alien is down."

Both men put their weapons back in their holsters and are dusting themselves off as the other four members of the crew come jogging into the viewing area.

Ms. Norata asks, "Are you two okay?"

Nathan answers, "Yes, we're fine thanks. He didn't want to give up. Foolish of him to attack two police officers who already have their weapons drawn."

Desiree adds, "I guess he'd rather be dead than go to prison."

Mr. Black says, "I guess so."

Nathan looks back down the path and says, "There's a clearing to the left about a hundred meters back. I'll have the ship land there, then we'll load the body and head home."

Nathan pushes the pickup button on his small remote wrist computer and walks back down the path towards the clearing.

Miles away at the aerodrome, the computer on board the police cruiser receives the pickup request and begins its automated launch procedures. The ship performs a perfect vertical takeoff, and then flies north, homing in on Nathan's wrist computer.

In just a few short minutes Nathan reaches the clearing and hears the police cruiser approaching. It clears the trees and begins its landing cycle, setting down in the center of the clearing. Nathan pushes a button on his small wrist computer to open the ramp. Once open, he walks up the ramp, heads to the medical bay and grabs a portable stretcher. Nathan takes the portable stretcher back to the viewing area and sets it down beside the body. Nathan and Mr. Bell grab the arms and Mr. Black and Mr. Nagata grab the legs.

Nathan says, "1... 2... 3... lift."

The four men pick the body up and place it on the stretcher. Then each man grabs a handle and lifts.

Mr. Black lets out a long low grunt and says, "Holy crap, this guy is heavy."

Nathan says, "Yeah, he must weigh about four hundred pounds."

It's quite a struggle to carry the heavy body all the way back down the path to the clearing. When they reach the ship, they carry the body up the ramp then head to the medical bay and place it in one of the two freezer drawers for transport back to Earth. Once the body is secure, everyone heads up to the bridge to prepare for takeoff.

After entering the bridge, Nathan sits down in his chair and says, "Ms. Arnoult, contact the local air traffic control tower and get us clearance for a vertical takeoff, then contact Solaris 5's space flight control and request clearance for space flight."

"Aye Captain."

"Mr. Bell, fire up the engines."

"Aye Captain."

The crew hears the jet engines spin up and start.

A minute later Desiree says, "Captain, the local air traffic control has given us clearance for a vertical takeoff, no traffic in the immediate area. Solaris 5's space flight control has also given us clearance for space flight."

"Thank you, Ms. Arnoult."

"Okay, Mr. Bell, take us up."

"Aye Captain."

Mr. Bell pushes the throttles half way open, and the ship begins to rise. When the ship reaches two hundred feet, he adjusts the thrust vectoring, and the ship starts to move forward. Mr. Bell rams the throttles wide open after which the ship accelerates and climbs rapidly, pushing the crew back in their seats. Several minutes after takeoff, the sky around the ship turns black as they near the edge of the planet's atmosphere. At this point Mr. Bell disengages the jet engines and closes the air intakes. He then engages the sub-light engines and rams the throttles wide open. The ship accelerates, almost violently, to achieve escape velocity.

The ship's computer announces in its female voice, “Now leaving Solaris 5's gravity. Artificial gravity plating is coming online.”

A few seconds later, Ms. Norata says, “Captain, there is an EDF ship dropping out of FTL about ten kilometers off our port bow.”

The crew looks out the front bridge windows just in time to see a bright blue flash of light and the appearance of a light cruiser.

Desiree says, “Captain, we have an incoming transmission from the cruiser.”

“On screen please, Ms. Arnoult.”

“Aye Captain.”

A young lieutenant commander appears on the view screen and says, “Greetings, I'm Lieutenant Commander Steven Walters, commanding officer of the EDF light cruiser, Atlanta. To whom do I have the pleasure of speaking?”

“I'm Captain Nathan Stone of the Planetary Police. Nice to meet you Commander Walters. Is there something we can help you with?”

“I'm sorry, did you say Captain Nathan Stone?”

“Yes.”

“Formerly Admiral Nathan Stone of the EDF?”

“The very same.”

"It is truly an honor to meet you, Captain Stone. Your tactics and mission logs are the foundation of everything taught at the academy."

"Thank you, Commander."

"You're welcome, Captain. Sir, we have been sent to investigate reports of a strange alien ship that is randomly appearing all over this sector. It is large, black with some green highlights, and it's shaped sort of like... well... a fish."

"I can't say I have seen it, Commander. I'm sure I would remember..."

Just then Ms. Norata interrupts Nathan yelling, "CAPTAIN, THERE IS A SHIP DROPPING OUT OF FTL RIGHT ON TOP OF THE ATLANTA!"

Through the bridge windows Nathan and his crew see a bright flash of blue light and the appearance of what seems to be the ship Commander Walters was just describing. The ship is shaped like an angel fish and is black as night save for a few green glowing highlights along some of its edges. It's a large ship, at least twice the size of the light cruiser.

The alien ship dropped out of FTL perpendicular to the cruiser, less than one hundred yards away. Extending down from the nose of the ship appears to be some sort of bright red plasma based bladed energy weapon.

On their view screen Nathan and his crew see Lieutenant Commander Walters turn to look out his port side bridge windows and a few of his bridge officers stand up before the transmission cuts off.

The alien ship dropped out of FTL so close and was moving so fast that the crew of the Atlanta had no time to react at all. It impacts the Atlanta amid ship, and the bladed energy weapon slices the cruiser in half like a hot knife cutting through butter. Its shields impact the two halves of the Atlanta and send them spinning off towards Nathan's cruiser and the planet.

Everyone is caught off-guard by the surprise attack and are in shock from what they have just witnessed. None of them have ever seen one ship cut another ship in half before.

Nathan's years of experience allow him to snap out of it quickly and he yells, "SHIELDS UP! EVASIVE MANEUVERS!"

Nathan yelling snaps the rest of the crew out of it and they respond to his orders.

Ms. Norata answers, "Aye Captain, shields up at full power."

Mr. Bell answers, "Aye Captain, evasive maneuvers," then rolls the ship to starboard and dives towards the planet.

Once they have cleared the path of the two halves of the Atlanta, Nathan says, "Mr. Bell, bring us around and get us into attack position."

"Aye Captain."

Mr. Bell swings the ship around so they can now see the belly of the alien spaceship in front of them.

"Ms. Norata, lock laser turrets on target and fire."

Ms. Norata says, "Aye Captain, laser turrets deployed and armed, target acquired.... firing."

From both sides of the ship's fuselage and underneath the ship erupts a series of powerful red laser blasts. The laser blasts impact on the alien ship's shields, no doubt they are draining power from their shields, but they aren't causing any visible damage yet.

"Ms. Norata, lock missiles on target and fire."

"Aye Captain, missiles locked.... firing."

Within a matter of seconds four missiles fire from the launchers hidden behind the doors on the leading edge of the ship's wings and go screaming off towards the alien ship.

"Ms. Norata, lock the Gatling lasers on target and fire."

“Aye Captain, Gatling lasers armed, target locked.... firing.”

The Gatling lasers in the wings of the police cruiser light up, each throwing sixty red laser blasts per second at the alien ship. The laser blasts impact on the ship’s shields, again draining power from their shields, but aren’t causing any visible damage yet.

Two seconds before the missiles reach their target the alien ship accelerates away rapidly and disappears in a bright blue flash of light as it enters FTL, leaving the missiles behind.

Disappointed, Nathan sits down in his chair and says, “Ms. Norata...”

“Aye Captain, detonating missiles now.”

Ms. Norata pushes a button on her console and all the missiles explode harmlessly out in space.

“Mr. Bell, swing us around so we can see the Atlanta.”

“Aye Captain.”

Mr. Bell brings the ship around so they can see the two halves of the light cruiser falling towards the planet. They can see large explosions inside both halves of the cruiser which cascade into massive explosions that vaporize the ship.

Nathan raises his hand to shield his eyes from the light generated by the explosions.

“Ms. Arnoult, contact EDF headquarters. I would like to speak to Admiral Daniels.”

“Aye Captain.”

“Mr. Black, plot a course for Earth.”

“Aye Captain, course laid in.”

“Mr. Bell, engage the FTL drive. Speed 14 TSL.”

“Aye Captain.”

The ship swings around and accelerates rapidly away from Solaris 5. Soon the crew sees the bright blue flash of light through the bridge windows as the ship enters FTL.

A few minutes later Mr. Bell says, "Captain, we have reached 14 TSL."

A minute later Desiree says, "Captain, I have Admiral Daniels for you."

"On screen please, Ms. Arnoult."

"Aye Captain."

Admiral Daniels appears on the main view screen and asks, "Captain Stone, to what do I owe this pleasure?"

"Admiral Daniels, unfortunately, sir, I am calling to report the loss of one of your ships, the light cruiser, Atlanta. She was attacked and cut in half by an alien ship. The subsequent explosions vaporized the ship and I regret to inform you that all hands were lost."

Admiral Daniels' face turns red, he grits his teeth in anger, stands up and says, "Thank you, Captain Stone. Would you report to EDF headquarters upon your return? Also, if you could send all sensor data and video starting five minutes before the attack, we will get to work analyzing it."

"Of course, Admiral."

"Thank you, Captain Stone. Daniels out."

The view screen goes dark.

Mr. Black turns his chair to look at Nathan and says, "Something tells me this is not the first time this has happened."

Nathan says, "Yes, I believe you are correct, Mr. Black."

"Ms. Norata, please transmit all sensor data and video footage of the attack as requested by the admiral."

"Aye Captain, transmitting now."

"Ms. Arnoult, get Carter on the line for me."

"Aye Captain."

A minute later Desiree says, "Captain, I have Carter for you now."

"On screen please, Ms. Arnoult."

"Aye Captain."

Carter appears on the main view screen, sitting behind his desk at Planetary Police headquarters. "Hey Nathan, how did you make out on Solaris 5?"

"Well, we found the alien that was causing all the ruckus, unfortunately he wouldn't come quietly. Stun blasts had no effect on him. Mr. Black and I had him cornered, he turned to attack us, and we had to put him down."

"That is unfortunate old buddy, but sometimes deadly force is necessary in this job. As long as you and your team are all okay."

"We're all fine thanks buddy. I have something else to report though."

"Oh, what's that?"

"My crew and I witnessed the unprovoked attack and destruction of the EDF light cruiser, Atlanta by an unknown alien vessel. The alien ship dropped out of FTL right on top of the cruiser and cut it in half with what looked to be some sort of plasma based bladed energy weapon. The alien ship jumped before we could do any damage with our weapons."

Carter is stunned and doesn't know what to say.

Nathan continues, "I spoke with Admiral Daniels and he requested that I report to him at EDF headquarters for a debrief as soon as we return. We've already sent him all our sensor logs and video footage of the attack."

Carter says, "I'll meet you at the landing pad and accompany you to the briefing."

"I thought you might want to come along. We're still four hours out at maximum speed. See you when we land. Later buddy."

"Safe travels people."

The view screen goes dark.

Nathan doesn't like the nature of the attack and not knowing anything about the capabilities of the attacking alien vessel, decides to err on the side of caution.

"Ms. Norata, cloak the ship. Rig for silent running."

"Aye Captain."

"Ms. Arnoult, maintain radio silence until we are on final approach to Earth."

"Aye Captain."

The mood aboard the police cruiser is more somber than usual. The crew is still trying to process the surprise attack, the loss of the Atlanta, and the death of over a thousand people right before their eyes.

Four hours later as the police cruiser approaches Earth, a series of beeps comes from his console and then Mr. Black says, "Captain, one minute until we arrive at Earth."

"Thank you, Mr. Black."

"Mr. Bell, drop us out of FTL."

"Aye Captain, dropping us out of FTL now."

The crew sees a bright blue flash of light as the police cruiser drops out of FTL and the Earth instantly appears through the bridge windows.

"Ms. Norata, disengage the cloaking device."

"Aye Captain, disengaging the cloaking device."

"Ms. Arnoult, contact Earth space flight control and request clearance for re-entry and then contact Seattle air traffic control, request an approach vector, and clearance to land on the helipad at Planetary Police headquarters."

"Aye Captain."

A few minutes later Ms. Arnoult says, "Captain, Earth space flight control has granted us clearance for re-entry. Seattle air traffic control has sent us an approach vector and granted us clearance for a vertical landing on the helipad at Planetary Police headquarters. I have sent the approach vector to Mr. Black's console."

"Thank you, Ms. Arnoult."

Mr. Black reviews the data and says, "Confirmed, approach vector laid in Captain."

"Thank you, Mr. Black."

"Mr. Bell, take us down."

"Aye Captain."

Mr. Bell noses the ship over and begins his descent into the atmosphere. The ship is descending over the Pacific Ocean, approaching the west coast of the United States. As they approach Seattle and the helipad at Planetary Police headquarters, Mr. Bell slows the ship down to a crawl and banks the ship to starboard slightly. Soon the ship is hovering at two hundred feet directly over the helipad. Mr. Bell pulls back on the throttles and the ship descends slowly. When the ship has dropped to about seventy-five feet Nathan gets up out of his chair and walks over to the port side bridge windows. Peering down he sees his friend Carter standing by the helipad waiting for them to land. When the ship has dropped to fifty feet, the landing gear comes down. A few moments later the wheels touch the ground and Mr. Bell shuts the engines down.

Nathan waves at Carter, then turns around and says, "Shut down all systems and then get the resupply underway. I'll be back soon."

In unison the crew answers, "Aye Captain."

Nathan exits the bridge and heads down to the lower bay. He opens the ramp and walks out onto the helipad to greet his best friend with a hug.

Motioning to the police car parked at the side of the helipad Carter says, “I’ve got a car waiting to take us to EDF headquarters for the debriefing with Admiral Daniels.”

Carter approaches the driver’s door and places his hand on the glass. A glowing green outline appears around his hand and a voice comes from the front of the car, “Recognize, Captain Carter Rayburn, access granted.”

The door opens, pivoting up towards the front of the car. Carter gets in and grabs the steering wheel, instantly all the cars systems come to life and his door closes. Nathan opens the passenger door and gets in. His door closes a few seconds after he sits down.

The car’s computerized voice says, “Hello Captain Rayburn, what is your destination?”

“EDF headquarters, Seattle.”

The car says, “Destination found and route laid in. Would you like me to drive?”

“Yes please.”

The car says, “Very well.”

The car begins to drive, pulling up to and then turning right onto the main street in front of police headquarters.

Carter asks Nathan, “So how big was this alien ship, anyway?”

“At least twice the size of a light cruiser. It’s big enough to take out our small to medium class ships, but it would be no match for our battle carriers. It’s not so much the size of the ship it’s their tactics that bother me. Dropping out of FTL right on top of a ship leaves no time for a captain to raise his defenses.”

After driving for about fifteen minutes, the police car turns into the parking lot at EDF headquarters and parks itself. Nathan and Carter get out of the car, head into the building, check in with security, and then take an elevator up to the top floor for their meeting with Admiral Daniels.

Admiral Daniels' aid meets them at the elevator and guides them to the conference room where the admiral is waiting.

As Nathan and Carter enter, the admiral stands up to greet them. Nathan shakes the admiral's hand and says, "Nice to see you again, Admiral."

"Likewise, Captain Stone."

"Admiral, you remember Captain Carter Rayburn."

The admiral shakes Carter's hand and says, "Yes, of course, nice to see you again, Captain Rayburn."

"Nice to see you as well, Admiral."

The admiral motions towards the conference room table and says, "Please have a seat, gentlemen."

They all take a seat at the table. From the control console the admiral dims the lights and activates the holographic display at the center of the table. The video captured by the cameras on Nathan's police cruiser starts to play. The video plays in its entirety from just before the alien ship drops out of FTL, to when it cuts the Atlanta in half and jumps to FTL again.

Carter is stunned, this is the first time he's seen the video of what happened. All he can say is, "Holy shit."

The admiral says, "Holy shit indeed, Captain Rayburn. The Atlanta is the third ship lost in that sector in the last three weeks. The first was a freighter, the second a passenger liner, and now the Atlanta. The big difference this time was you, Captain Stone. There were no witnesses to what happened to the other two ships. All we have is their maydays and some yelling about an attacking ship before their transmissions cut off. After reviewing your sensor logs and videos we are confident that this alien ship is responsible for all three incidents."

Nathan asks the admiral, "Have your people been able to determine whose ship that is?"

"Actually, yes Captain Stone. We are positive because of the aquatic design of the ship that the race responsible are the Xandurians. The ship shows design elements similar to the Xandurian ships already known to us, but this seems to be a new class of ship. We think because the targets are getting bigger with each attack that this is a prototype weapon they are testing."

Nathan says, "What do we know about the Xandurians, Admiral?"

"Well, Captain Stone, we know that Xandur is an Earth type planet. Ninety percent of its surface is covered in water so the inhabitants are aquatic in nature, though they can breathe air and live on land."

The admiral pushes a button on the control console and the hologram changes to display a picture of a few Xandurians.

Nathan immediately recognizes the species as the same as the deceased troublemaker from Solaris 5 that is in the refrigeration unit in his ship's medical bay.

"Uh Admiral, I have a deceased Xandurian in one of the refrigeration units in my ship's medical bay. He was causing problems on Solaris 5 and refused to surrender when we cornered him."

"Well, isn't that an amazing coincidence? Please let me know when you have completed your paperwork and closed the file on this case. I will arrange to have the body picked up and brought over to our science division for an extensive examination. We need to learn all we can about them."

"Of course, Admiral."

The admiral continues, "After the Sulari incident our intelligence sources discovered that another species hired the Sulari to steal a supply of the ore from Trynx 3 no doubt to power a time machine. We believe that species to be the Xandurians. We believe they are the brains behind the whole thing. The Sulari weren't smart enough to build a time machine, but it is possible that the Xandurians are."

Just then the intercom buzzes. The admiral pushes a button on the console and says, "Yes, what is it?"

The admiral's aid's voice comes on and says, "Admiral, there is a priority one message from Colonel Williamson on Trynx 3, sir."

"Oh, that can't be good news. Put it through in here."

"Yes Admiral."

The hologram switches off briefly and then Colonel Williamson's form appears at the center of the table.

"Colonel Williamson, something tells me this is not good news."

"You would be correct, Admiral Daniels. We have had a serious breach in security in the surface compound."

"Oh?"

"Yes Admiral, one of the civilian contractors sabotaged the security systems, knocked out several guards, broke into the armory, stole a crate of the ore, and then stole a transport. He evaded our fighter patrol and jumped into FTL before the cruisers in orbit could stop him."

"Which civilian contractor?"

"John Tisdale, sir. He is the lead systems design engineer for the planetary monitoring system."

"All right, Colonel Williamson, since he is a civilian, I will get the Planetary Police to start an investigation. I happen to be meeting with two of their best officers right now. No doubt they will be heading your way shortly. Daniels out."

The admiral shuts the holographic display down, looks at Nathan and says, "Well, Captain, it looks as if I have a case for you. How fast can you get under way?"

"Within the hour, Admiral."

"Excellent, go get him and bring back that ore."

Nathan and Carter stand, and out of respect for their former commanding officer they snap to attention, salute him, and say, "Yes Admiral."

"I don't think I need to tell you how dangerous it would be if that ore were to fall into the wrong hands. Good hunting gentlemen and be careful. Who knows where that alien ship will appear next."

Nathan nods and then he and Carter leave the conference room, take the elevator down to the ground floor and head back to their police car. When they get in the car, Carter instructs the car to drive them back to Planetary Police headquarters. The car begins to drive, pulling up to and then turning left onto the main street in front of EDF headquarters.

As the car begins the trip back to police headquarters Carter looks at Nathan and says, "Are you thinking what I'm thinking?"

"How did an alien species get one of our own to turn against us?"

"Yeah."

Both men state in unison, "Blackmail."

Carter asks, "You mind if I tag along on this one, old buddy?"

"Not at all, my friend, we could use the extra set of hands on this one."

When they arrive back at police headquarters, they see Nathan's crew finishing up the resupply of the ship. Carter instructs the police car to park beside the helipad. Nathan and Carter get out and walk over to the ship where Mr. Black is standing with a tablet going through the manifest as they load the supplies.

Nathan says, “How soon before we can take off, Mr. Black?”

“About half an hour, Captain.”

“Very well, Mr. Black. Half an hour it is.”

Nathan turns to Carter and says, “Better go grab your gear.”

Carter says, “I always keep an emergency go bag packed in my office. I’ll go grab it and my gear and be back in fifteen minutes.”

Nathan gives him a quick nod and Carter runs off towards police headquarters.

Mr. Black asks, “Captain Rayburn’s joining us on this one, sir?”

“Yes, we could use his help on this mission. Show him to the spare cabin beside yours when he gets back. I’ll be on the bridge.”

“Aye Captain.”

“Oh and have the body in our medical bay transferred to the morgue and then send a message to Admiral Daniels at EDF headquarters to let him know he can have the body picked up from there.”

“Aye Captain.”

Nathan heads up the ramp into the ship and makes his way up to the bridge. He uses the computer console at the tactical station to pull up the personnel file on John Tisdale and starts reading.

After about half an hour, the rest of the crew files into the bridge, including Carter.

When Desiree has taken her seat Nathan says, “Ms. Arnoult, contact Seattle air traffic control and request clearance for takeoff and then contact Earth space flight control and request clearance for space flight."

"Aye Captain."

"Mr. Bell, fire up the engines."

"Aye Captain."

The crew hears the jet engines spin up and start.

Moments later Desiree says, "Captain, Seattle air traffic control has granted us clearance for a vertical takeoff and Earth space flight control has granted us clearance for space flight. Both report no traffic in the immediate area."

"Thank you, Ms. Arnoult."

"Mr. Bell, take us up."

"Aye Captain."

Mr. Bell pushes the throttles half way open, and the ship begins to rise. When the ship reaches two hundred feet, he adjusts the thrust vectoring, and the ship starts to move forward. There is no seat for Carter to sit down in, so he is standing behind Nathan's chair holding on to the bulkhead above. Keeping this in mind, Mr. Bell accelerates and climbs more gradually instead of ramming the throttles wide open. Several minutes after takeoff, the sky around the ship turns black as they near the edge of the planet's atmosphere. At this point Mr. Bell disengages the jet engines and closes the air intakes. He then engages the sub-light engines and pushes the throttles up. The ship accelerates and soon achieves escape velocity.

The ship's computer announces in its female voice, "Now leaving Earth's gravity. Artificial gravity plating is coming online."

As soon as they break orbit Nathan says, "Mr. Black, plot a course for Trynx 3."

"Aye Captain, course laid in."

"Mr. Bell, engage the FTL drive. Speed 14 TSL."

"Aye Captain."

The ship accelerates rapidly away from Earth, and soon the crew sees the bright blue flash of light through the bridge windows as the ship enters FTL.

A few minutes later Mr. Bell says, "Captain, we have reached 14 TSL. Estimated time to Trynx 3 is six hours."

"Thank you, Mr. Bell."

Nathan activates the main view screen and displays John Tisdale's record and photograph.

"This man is the reason we are heading to Trynx 3. John Tisdale is the lead systems design engineer for the company that was awarded the contract to implement a multi-layered planetary monitoring system on Trynx 3."

"He was posted there six months ago to get the system designed, installed and operational. The man is a certified genius in many respects."

"The problem is last night he went rogue. He sabotaged the security systems, knocked out several of the guards, broke into the armory, stole a crate of the Trynx 3 ore, and then stole a transport. He evaded the fighter patrol and jumped in to FTL before the cruisers in orbit could stop him."

"Our job is to figure out why he did this, then we have to go find him and bring him and the ore back to Trynx 3."

Ms. Norata says, "That makes no sense. The man is a genius, and he's never done a bad thing in his life. Why would he suddenly go rogue and steal some of the ore?"

Carter says, "Well we came up with one possibility. He's being blackmailed. Someone is forcing him to steal the ore and deliver it to them."

Nathan says, "The only other real possibility is they paid him an unbelievable amount of money to steal it."

Desiree asks, "How much money would it take for a man to betray his entire race?"

Mr. Black says, "For some people, probably a lot less than you think."

Mr. Bell says, "This guy doesn't seem like the type though."

Nathan says, "I agree."

## CHAPTER 3 - TRAGEDY

Six hours later as the police cruiser approaches Trynx 3, a series of beeps comes from his console and then Mr. Black says, “Captain, one minute until we arrive at Trynx 3.”

“Thank you, Mr. Black.”

“Mr. Bell, drop us out of FTL.”

“Aye Captain, dropping us out of FTL now.”

The crew sees a bright blue flash of light as the police cruiser drops out of FTL, and Trynx 3 instantly appears through the bridge windows.

Carter, Nathan and his crew are amazed at the huge military presence safeguarding the planet. They see the web of defense satellites surrounding the planet, they see the large military space station, and they see a fleet of over a hundred ships. The fleet is comprised of two battle carriers, twenty heavy cruisers, fifty light cruisers and fifty destroyers spread all about in orbit of the planet. At that moment there are at least six full squadrons of F-114 Tomcats split into pairs patrolling the outer edge of the defensive sphere around the planet. The defenses that the EDF put in place are sufficient to defend the planet against an all-out alien attack until the bulk of the fleet can arrive from Earth to back them up.

Nathan says, “Ms. Arnoult, contact the station and request clearance through the defense satellites and then contact air traffic control at the surface compound and request clearance to land.”

“Aye Captain.”

After a few minutes Desiree says, “Captain, we have clearance through the defense satellites and clearance to land on helipad one in the compound.”

“Thank you, Ms. Arnoult.”

"Mr. Bell, take us down."

"Aye Captain."

Mr. Bell noses the ship over and begins his approach. They pass through the web of defense satellites and enter the upper atmosphere. The ride gets a little bumpy as they begin their descent and since there is no seat for him on the bridge, Carter grabs onto the bulkhead above to steady himself. Luckily the turbulence doesn't last for long and soon the ship is dropping into the lower atmosphere. The ship is descending towards the compound from the west. As they approach the compound, Mr. Bell slows the ship down to a crawl and banks the ship to starboard, turning it ninety degrees to line it up with the helipad. Soon the ship is hovering at two hundred feet directly over the helipad. Mr. Bell pulls back on the throttles and the ship descends slowly. When the ship has dropped to fifty feet, the landing gear comes down. Moments later the wheels touch the ground and Mr. Bell shuts the engines down.

Nathan stands up and says, "Nice smooth landing, Mr. Bell."

"Thank you, Captain."

"All right everyone, shut everything down and let's go."

After shutting all the ship's systems down, they all exit the bridge and make their way down to the lower bay. Nathan opens the ramp, and the crew walks out onto the helipad. They are met by the compound's chief of security, Lieutenant Marcus Lee.

The lieutenant shakes Nathan's hand and says, "Captain Stone, welcome to Trynx 3. If you and your crew will follow me, I will take you to see the base commander, Colonel Williamson."

"Thank you, Lieutenant, lead the way."

The lieutenant guides them across the compound to the command center's main entrance and up to the second floor conference room.

When everyone is in the conference room the lieutenant says, "Please, everyone, have a seat and the colonel will join us shortly."

Everyone sits down at the conference table to wait for Colonel Williamson to join them. They don't have to wait long however as the colonel walks into the conference room about a minute later. The lieutenant stands and snaps to attention. Carter, Nathan and his crew stand to greet the colonel.

The colonel approaches Nathan, shakes his hand and says, "Captain Stone, it's an honor to meet you."

"Thank you, Colonel Williamson, it's a pleasure to meet you, sir. My team and I stand ready to begin our investigation and track down the perpetrator."

"Very well, Captain, my lieutenant will brief you on what we have so far."

Everyone in the conference room takes their seats, and the lieutenant activates the holographic display in the center of the table. The lieutenant starts by bringing up a rotating holographic image of John Tisdale.

"This is John Tisdale. Mr. Tisdale was the lead systems design engineer for the company that was awarded the contract to implement a multi-layered planetary monitoring system here on Trynx 3. Mr. Tisdale arrived on Trynx 3 six months ago and was almost ready to bring the monitoring system online before he went rogue."

The lieutenant brings up an image showing the highlights of John Tisdale's file.

"Mr. Tisdale has no prior criminal record of any kind. He graduated from MIT with a master's degree in engineering and then went to Cornell and graduated with a master's degree in computer sciences. He is considered a genius with an IQ somewhere in the one-sixty range. He is married and has two children back on Earth."

The lieutenant brings up a 3D map of the compound showing what they have surmised as the route Tisdale took through the compound.

"Since Mr. Tisdale took down our security systems and cameras, we have had to piece this together from physical evidence."

"As you can see here, Mr. Tisdale entered the inner compound through this door after knocking out a guard and taking his tactical helmet, night vision and pulse rifle. He worked his way around the compound keeping close to the outer wall and hiding behind the various crates, barrels, and parked vehicles along the way."

"When he got close to the armory, he crawled underneath one of the mining trucks where he stunned the two guards that were standing watch at the door. He dragged one of the guards over and placed his hand on the biometric scanner to open the door into the armory."

"After dragging both guards inside the armory, he located the lock up where the time ore was stored and blasted the gate open with the pulse rifle."

"He took one crate of the ore, exited the armory, and made his way over to the helipad where he stole a standard military transport vehicle using his emergency evacuation training."

"After takeoff, Mr. Tisdale managed to evade two of our F-114 Tomcats, achieved orbit, and entered FTL before the heavy cruisers in orbit could intercept him."

"We have video footage of his escape from our security team's body cams, the Tomcats, and from the heavy cruisers in orbit."

The lieutenant plays the videos for Carter, Nathan and his crew. They watch as the transport lifts off from the compound and takes off across the sky, they watch as the transport evades being shot down by the Tomcats, they watch as the transport and the pursuing Tomcats climb from the planet up towards the heavy cruisers in orbit, and finally they watch the transport accelerate away, jump into FTL, and disappear in a bright blue flash of light.

The lieutenant stops the video playback and says, “Once we knew who it was that had stolen the transport a quick search of his quarters revealed that he had left a video log explaining his actions.”

The lieutenant plays the video showing John Tisdale sitting in his quarters.

“Hello, I’m John Tisdale and this video should explain my actions whether I have gotten away or not.”

“A few days ago, an alien claiming to have kidnapped my wife and children, contacted me and said if I didn’t steal a crate of the Trynx 3 ore and bring it to him, he would kill my family. He also instructed me not to tell anyone about this. If I did, he would know, and he would kill my family.”

“However, after a quick scan of my quarters I found no evidence of any surveillance equipment, so I risked creating this video using my personal comm tablet with the network shut off to avoid any possibility of discovery.”

“They have instructed me to rendezvous with a ship in orbit of the fourth planet in the Minar system. The transport’s FTL drive is limited to 5 TSL so it will take me five days to get to there.” 7

“That gives you five days to find my family, rescue them and send someone to intercept me before I reach the rendezvous coordinates. Please hurry.”

The hologram fades to black and disappears.

Nathan looks around at Carter and his crew and then back at Colonel Williamson and says, “Well that was easy wasn’t it?”

“Do you believe him, Captain Stone?”

“I’m not sure Colonel, I’d like to verify a few things before I say either way. Have you been able to track the transport?”

"Yes, the transponder is active and so far, he's heading towards the Minar system. How do you plan on proceeding, Captain?"

"Well to start with I will have someone check on his wife and kids, verify they exist, and try to locate them. I'd also like to run his video through one of our programs that checks for non-verbal cues. It's sort of a lie detector program for video messages."

"Very well, Captain, the lieutenant here will assist you with whatever you need. Keep me informed of your progress."

"Excellent, thank you, Colonel, and I will, sir."

Everyone at the table stands, the colonel walks out of the conference room and heads back to his office.

Nathan looks at the lieutenant and says, "Lieutenant, I'll be needing a copy of that video."

The lieutenant holds up a small optical disk and says, "Way ahead of you, Captain Stone."

Nathan smiles, nods and says, "Excellent, thank you, Lieutenant."

Nathan looks over at Carter and his crew and says, "All right, everyone, let's get back to the ship. We have a lot to do."

Carter acknowledges by nodding his head.

Nathan's crew all answer with, "Aye Captain," and then everyone files out the conference room door one at a time.

They make their way back to the ship and head up to the bridge. The crew takes their seats and Nathan issues orders while Carter stands back and observes Nathan's crew work like a well-oiled machine.

"Ms. Norata, take the disk and run the video through the body language analyzer to see if Mr. Tisdale is telling the truth or not."

Ms. Norata says, "Aye Captain," takes the disk from Nathan and plugs it into the reader in her console.

"Ms. Arnoult, contact headquarters and have someone verify that his wife and children exist, and if they do, have them send someone to investigate Mr. Tisdale's home on Earth to check on them."

"Aye Captain."

Nathan pushes a button on the console on his chair activating the comm system and says, "Trynx 3 base, this is Captain Nathan Stone, patch me through to Lieutenant Lee."

The communications officer on duty in the base replies, "Of course, Captain Stone, one minute for Lieutenant Lee."

A few moments later Lieutenant Lee comes on, "Captain Stone, this is Lieutenant Lee. What can I do for you, sir?"

"Lieutenant, would you send the transponder code and the navigational data for Mr. Tisdale's transport to my navigator?"

"Of course, Captain, transmitting the data now."

A few seconds later Mr. Black says, "Captain, I have received Lieutenant Lee's transmission, pulling it up now."

Nathan says, "Thank you, Lieutenant."

"You're welcome, Captain Stone."

"Stone out."

Nathan pushes the button on his console to shut down the comm system and says, "Mr. Black, activate the holographic projector, let's see it."

"Aye Captain."

Mr. Black activates the holographic projector and a star map appears with Trynx 3 at the bottom left and Minar 4 at the top right. Also displayed is a thin white line showing the transport's flight path between the two planets and moving red dot with the transport's transponder code next to it about one fifth of the way along the path.

Nathan looks at Carter and says, “So far it looks like he is telling the truth. What do you think, Carter?”

“Too early to tell, Nathan. We’ll have to wait and see.”

Nathan says, “Agreed. Good thing his ship is limited to 5 TSL. Even though he has about an eighteen hour head start on us, it won’t take us long to catch up to him at 14 TSL. Wouldn’t you agree, Mr. Black?”

“Yes Captain, by my calculations if we leave now, we can catch up to him in a little over an hour.”

“Well then we better get going, hadn’t we?”

“Yes Captain.”

“Ms. Arnoult, contact Trynx 3 air traffic control and request clearance for takeoff.”

“Aye Captain.”

“Mr. Bell, fire up the engines.”

“Aye Captain.”

The crew hears the jet engines spin up and start.

Moments later Desiree says, “Captain, Trynx 3 air traffic control says clearance for vertical takeoff is granted, no traffic in the immediate area.”

“Thank you, Ms. Arnoult.”

“Mr. Bell, take us up.”

“Aye Captain.”

Mr. Bell pushes the throttles half way open, and the ship rises. When the ship reaches two hundred feet Mr. Bell adjusts the thrust vectoring, and the ship moves forward. Once again there is no seat for Carter to sit down in, so he is standing behind Nathan’s chair holding on to the bulkhead above. Keeping this in mind, Mr. Bell accelerates and climbs more gradually instead of ramming the throttles wide open. Several minutes after takeoff, the sky around the ship turns black as they near the edge of the planet's atmosphere. At this point Mr. Bell disengages the jet engines and closes the air intakes. He then engages the sub-light engines and pushes the throttles up. The ship accelerates and soon achieves escape velocity.

The ship's computer announces in its female voice, "Now leaving Trynx 3's gravity. Artificial gravity plating is coming online."

"Mr. Black, plot a course to intercept Mr. Tisdale's transport."

"Aye Captain, course laid in."

"Okay, Mr. Bell, engage the FTL drive and let's go get him. Speed 14 TSL."

"Aye Captain, engaging the FTL drive now."

The ship accelerates rapidly away from Trynx 3 and soon the crew sees the bright blue flash of light through the bridge windows as the ship enters FTL.

After a few minutes Mr. Bell says, "Captain, we have reached 14 TSL. Estimated time to intercept Mr. Tisdale's transport is sixty-five minutes."

"Thank you, Mr. Bell."

A few minutes later they receive a signal from Planetary Police headquarters.

Desiree says, "Captain, we have an incoming transmission from Planetary Police headquarters."

"On screen please, Ms. Arnoult."

"Aye Captain."

The main view screen at the front of the bridge activates displaying the newly appointed police chief, David Tanner sitting at his desk.

Nathan says, "Chief Tanner, this is an unexpected pleasure."

"Captain Stone, I wanted to bring you up to speed on what we have found out about Mr. Tisdale's family."

"What have you found, sir?"

"Mr. Tisdale was telling the truth, he has a wife and two children that live in a nice neighborhood in Detroit. When we sent someone to check on them, we found that the door had been broken in and there were signs of a struggle inside. We pulled footage from their home security system showing four Xandurians forcing their way in and taking his wife and children."

The chief hits a button on his desk console and the security video plays in a smaller window in the bottom right corner of the view screen.

The chief continues, "As you can see here, after the Xandurians have the family subdued they take them out to a delivery vehicle and drive off."

The security video cuts off at that point.

"Once we had the timeline and the image of the vehicle, we were able to track them using the city's security surveillance system and security satellites."

"The Xandurians took them to a rundown house in an old abandoned neighborhood on the east side of Detroit. We sent a surveillance team to the house to set up infrared cameras and sure enough there were seven heat signatures inside."

The chief hits a button on his console again and the high definition infrared pictures display in the form of a slideshow in a smaller window in the bottom right corner of the view screen.

"As you can see in these detailed photos, there are four Xandurians in the house, two in the front room and two in the back room with an adult human female and two human children."

"We've dispatched our best SWAT team to Detroit to extract the hostages and take out the aliens. They arrived on site a short while ago, assessed the situation, deployed their team and four snipers around the house and they are now ready to execute their plan. I will now switch you to the tactical team leader's live video stream from inside his mobile command unit."

The view screen switches to show the multi-screen display inside the mobile command unit. Nathan and his crew can see the infrared view of the house, the helmet cams of each of the team members, and the views through each of the snipers' x-ray scopes. Through these high-powered x-ray scopes, the snipers can see the structure of the walls, the layout and contents of the rooms, the aliens' skeletons, and the thin outline of their bodies. These scopes help them avoid anything that may change the trajectory of the bullet, accurately target the aliens, and guarantee a kill shot. These scopes mounted on high-powered fifty caliber sniper rifles, in the hands of a trained sniper are a deadly combination. The bad guys have nowhere to hide anymore.

Nathan and his team can also hear what the tactical team's commanding officer is saying. He orders one of his technical support people to prep and release a fly sized drone to go into the house for a set of eyes and ears inside the house. He also orders his technical team to jam all civilian communication frequencies in a five-block radius.

A few minutes go by before Nathan and his team hear the technical support person report he has launched the fly drone and that it is streaming video now. The center screen in the display changes from the infrared view of the house to the fly drone's video feed. The fly drone makes its way into the front room of the house where it perches itself on a ceiling light looking down on the room. The video feed shows the two Xandurians walking around the room, armed with pulse rifles. The technician enables the translator so everyone watching the video stream can now hear the two Xandurians discussing how they should kill the humans and get out of there.

The fly drone takes off again, flies into the back room and perches on a wall shelf. The video feed shows the other two Xandurians standing just inside the door, also armed with pulse rifles. It also shows the mother and the two children sitting on the floor, leaning against the back wall. These two Xandurians are discussing how much longer they will have to stay there to guard these disgusting humans.

Nathan and his team hear one of the technical support people in the tactical command center say they have positively identified the human hostages as the Tisdales.

Just then there is a commotion from the front room. The two Xandurians from the front room run into the back room yelling about the comm channels being down.

The tactical commander orders his snipers to select their targets and take aim. All four feeds from the snipers' scopes show the crosshairs in the center of the aliens' heads.

One alien yells they should kill the humans and get out of there. The other aliens agree. They turn and raise their pulse rifles towards Mrs. Tisdale and her two children.

The tactical commander orders his team to take them out.

Nathan and his team don't hear the concussion of the high-powered rifles being fired. All they see on the video feeds from the sniper scopes are the aliens' heads exploding as all four large caliber bullets find their marks and the bodies dropping to the floor lifeless and unmoving.

On the video feed from the fly drone, they see a disgusting mess they are glad they don't have to clean up.

The rest of the tactical team burst into the house, clearing it room by room until they get to the back room where they find the four dead aliens and three live humans that are going into shock. One of the tactical team members in the house gets on the radio and calls for the medical teams to come in to tend to the survivors.

Everyone is happy that Mrs. Tisdale and her two children are alive and will be okay.

The view screen switches from the tactical command unit back to Police Chief Tanner.

Chief Tanner says, “Captain Stone, contact Mr. Tisdale and let him know he can stop, his family is safe.”

Nathan replies, “Yes sir, I will keep you posted. Stone out.”

The main view screen powers down and Nathan says, “Ms. Arnoult, setup a broadcast to all military channels.”

“Aye Captain, broadcast ready.”

“Attention, John Tisdale, this is Captain Nathan Stone of Earth’s Planetary Police, please respond.”

Nathan waits for about ten seconds. There is no response, so he tries again.

“Attention, John Tisdale, this is Captain Nathan Stone of Earth’s Planetary Police, please respond.”

This time there is a response.

“This is John Tisdale.”

“Mr. Tisdale, Captain Stone here. I’m contacting you to let you know your family is safe and well. Drop your ship out of FTL and wait for our arrival.”

“How do I know you’re telling me the truth? How do I know you’re not telling me this just to stop me?”

“We found your video message, and then we used security footage and satellites to find where the Xandurians took your family. I watched the tactical team rescue them myself. Besides, if I wanted to stop you it wouldn’t be that difficult.”

“Oh? How is that now?”

“You forgot to turn off your ship’s transponder. You’re broadcasting your location to the entire EDF fleet. We’ve been tracking you the whole time. My ship is a lot faster than yours and heavily armed, I could have easily taken you out. So, trust me and drop your ship out of FTL."

There are a few moments of silence.

"Mr. Tisdale, are you reading me?"

"Yes, Captain Stone, I read you. Dropping out of FTL now."

"Very good, Mr. Tisdale. Sit tight, we'll be there in less than five minutes to escort you back to Trynx 3."

"Okay, Captain Stone. See you soon. Tisdale out."

"Ms. Norata, can you confirm he has dropped out of FTL?"

"Aye Captain, he's stopped."

"Excellent, thank you, Ms. Norata."

A few minutes later a series of beeps comes from his console and then Mr. Black says, "Captain, one minute to Mr. Tisdale's coordinates."

Nathan says, "Thank you, Mr. Black."

"Ms. Norata, anything else on the sensors?"

"No Captain, nothing else on sensors, just Mr. Tisdale's ship."

"Thank you, Ms. Norata."

"Mr. Bell, drop us out of FTL."

"Aye Captain, dropping us out of FTL now."

The crew sees a bright blue flash of light through the bridge windows as the police cruiser drops out of FTL.

Looking out the bridge windows they can see Mr. Tisdale's transport about half a kilometer off the port bow.

Nathan says, "Ms. Arnoult, open a channel."

"Aye Captain, channel open."

"Mr. Tisdale, this is Captain Stone. We just arrived at your coordinates and are approaching from your starboard side aft."

Mr. Tisdale gets up out of his chair and looks out the starboard side windows. He activates his comm system and says, "Roger that, I see your ship, Captain Stone. By chance do you have an update on my family? Are they okay?"

"Yes, we received an update a few minutes ago Mr. Tisdale. Your wife and children will be fine. They have a few cuts and bruises, they were hungry, and a little dehydrated, nothing serious."

"Does my wife understand everything that happened?"

"Yes, Mr. Tisdale, our people explained that they were kidnapped to force you to bring the Xandurians some of the Trynx 3 ore. She has also been informed that we have been in contact with you, that you stopped and that you'll be home soon."

"You mean I won't be charged with anything? I won't be going to prison?"

"I can't say for sure, Mr. Tisdale, but considering the circumstances, I highly doubt it."

"That's good to know, thank you, Captain Stone."

"You're welcome, Mr. Tisdale. Now how about we turn these ships around and head back to Trynx 3?"

Ms. Norata interrupts the conversation and yells, "CAPTAIN, THERE IS A SHIP DROPPING OUT OF FTL RIGHT ON TOP OF US!"

The Xandurian ship with its bladed energy weapon deployed appears immediately off the starboard side of the police cruiser and is closing the distance fast.

Without waiting for an order from Nathan, Mr. Bell punches the RCS thrusters and drops the ship straight down on the Z axis. Mr. Bell's reaction time was incredibly fast, but he didn't have enough time to clear the weapon. The tip of the bladed energy weapon slices through the roof of the bridge, cutting a large gash in the hull. The bridge depressurizes, violently venting atmosphere into space causing a windstorm effect inside the ship. Carter, who was standing behind Nathan, turns to grab onto Ms. Norata's console, but he is not quick enough. The windstorm picks him up like a piece of paper.

Nathan reaches up to grab his hand and yells, "CARTER!"

Nathan is not able to grab Carter's hand. Carter is ejected through the hole and out into space along with numerous small items that were on the bridge. A few seconds later the computer snaps on an emergency force field sealing the hull and preventing the rest of the atmosphere from escaping.

Nathan feels like he's just been kicked in the stomach. He puts his face in his hands for a few seconds and screams out in anguish. He quickly realizes that the grieving will have to wait. His ship and his crew are still in danger. At this point, anger wells up inside him and it's about to boil over.

Nathan becomes enraged and yells, "MR. BELL, COME ABOUT AND BRING THE WEAPONS TO BEAR ON THAT SHIP!"

"Aye Captain."

As Mr. Bell maneuvers them behind the alien ship and into attack position.

Nathan yells, "MS. NORATA, SHIELDS UP, TARGET THAT SHIP AND FIRE EVERYTHING WE'VE GOT! BLOW THAT SON OF A BITCH STRAIGHT TO HELL! FIRE AT WILL!"

"Aye Captain, shields up, laser turrets deployed and armed, target acquired.... firing."

From both sides of the ship's fuselage and underneath the ship erupts a series of powerful red laser blasts. The laser blasts impact on the alien ship's shields, draining power.

"Gatling lasers armed, target acquired.... firing."

The Gatling lasers in the wings of the police cruiser light up throwing sixty red laser blasts per second at the alien ship.

The laser blasts impact on the alien ship's shields, draining more power.

"Particle beam weapons armed, target acquired.... firing."

From the tips of the police cruiser's wings erupts two long, red, sparkling beams that impact on the alien ship's shields, draining even more power.

"Missiles locked.... firing."

Within a matter of seconds four missiles fire from the launchers hidden behind the doors on the leading edge of the ship's wings and go screaming off towards the alien ship. A few seconds later the missiles impact on the alien ship's shields and explode.

The alien ship performs some evasive maneuvers, but it is a great deal bigger than the police cruiser and nowhere near as fast or maneuverable, so Mr. Bell is having no problem staying right behind them. None of the alien ship's weapons are able to target the police cruiser where it is situated, a potentially deadly flaw in the design of the alien ship. The unrelenting bombardment from all three of the police cruiser's energy weapons is putting a massive strain on the alien ship's shields.

Ms. Norata says, "Their shields aren't going to take much more of this. I'm going to launch another three missile salvos."

A second later, the first salvo of four missiles fire from the launchers in the leading edge of the ship's wings and go screaming off towards the alien ship. Ten seconds later a second salvo of four missiles fire. Ten seconds after that a third salvo of four missiles fire. There are now twelve missiles closing rapidly on the alien ship.

The first salvo of missiles hits the alien ship's shields and explode. Immediately after that the blasts from the laser turrets, the Gatling lasers and the particle beam weapons impact on the alien ship's hull, blowing pieces off and slicing through the outer hull.

Ms. Norata says, "Their shields are down."

The other two missile salvos reach their target and destroy two of the starboard side thrusters on the rear of the alien ship.

The energy weapons continue to cause major damage especially the Gatling lasers. Their high cyclic rate is chewing the alien ship's hull to pieces.

The bladed energy weapon on the alien ship shuts down, the lights and the thrusters flicker on and off.

Nathan says, "They're having power issues. Target their reactor core with the particle beam weapons and fire."

"Aye Captain."

Before Ms. Norata can target their reactor core and fire, the alien ship accelerates away rapidly, enters FTL, and disappears in a bright blue flash of light.

Nathan falls back into his chair, slams his fist down on his armrest and yells, "GOD DAMMIT!"

He takes a few seconds to compose himself and says, "Mr. Bell, bring us back alongside Mr. Tisdale's transport."

"Aye Captain."

"Ms. Arnoult, send a message to Admiral Daniels. Tell him we have sustained damage to our outer hull that prevents us from jumping into FTL and request he send a cruiser to pick us up."

"Aye Captain."

Nathan gets up and heads towards the bridge door pausing for a moment to look at Desiree. Desiree stands and puts her hand on his forearm. She can see the anger, pain and sorrow in his eyes.

Desiree opens her mouth to say she is sorry about Carter, but Nathan cuts her off, "I'm going to go get Carter," then walks off the bridge.

Nathan makes his way to the shuttle bay and preps the shuttle for launch. He puts on a space suit, enters the shuttle, and sits down in the pilot's chair. He closes the door, fires up the engines, and opens the shuttle bay doors. Nathan pushes the throttles up a little and the shuttle lifts off the deck. He then nudges it forward towards the shuttle bay doors. A few seconds later the shuttle passes through the atmospheric force field and out into space. Nathan pulls the shuttle up and points the nose in the general direction that Carter would have been thrown by the sudden depressurization. Nathan pushes the throttles about half way open and scans for his friend's body. Carter has a good head start on him and was moving fast. It could take Nathan a little while to catch up to him.

Nathan feels very anxious about finding and possibly saving Carter even though he knows it is irrational to think Carter might still be alive. He will hold on to hope until he finds Carter and sees with his own eyes that his best friend from the age of five is gone.

After about fifteen minutes, a small blip appears on the edge of the shuttle's scanners about a hundred kilometers away. The object is vectoring away from Nathan's shuttle, so he changes his course to intercept it and increases his speed. Nathan is gaining on what he is hoping is Carter, if it isn't, Nathan will have to declare him as lost. If this isn't him, finding his body would be like trying to find a needle in a haystack where the haystack is a thousand times the size of Mount Everest.

Nathan anxiously says to himself, "Come on, come on, come on."

A few minutes later Nathan catches up to the object on his scanners, so he decelerates and matches the object's speed. He turns on all the exterior lights on the shuttle and scans around the shuttle. Finally, he spots the object and thankfully it is Carter. Nathan feels a little relief having found Carter but is struggling to keep his anxiety from turning into panic. He can't get Carter into the shuttle soon enough.

Nathan maneuvers the shuttle so it is just in front of Carter and shuts down the engines. Using the thrusters, he spins the shuttle ninety degrees to starboard, so the shuttle is side slipping and the side door is now lined up with Carter. Nathan puts on his space helmet, turns on his magnetic boots, vents the atmosphere of the shuttle and turns off the artificial gravity. He walks back to and opens the side door. He sees his best friend is just out of reach outside the door. Nathan walks back up to the front of the shuttle and fires the port thrusters for a split second, slowing the shuttle down ever so slightly causing Carter to gain on it. Nathan walks back to the open door, reaches out, grabs Carter's arm and pulls him inside the shuttle. He gently guides him down to the floor then turns and closes the door.

Nathan's anxiety is replaced by gut wrenching sadness as he looks into Carter's frozen eyes and realizes that his best friend is gone.

Nathan walks up to the front of the shuttle, turns the artificial gravity back on, shuts off his magnetic boots, replenishes the atmosphere inside the shuttle, and removes his helmet. He sits down in the pilot's chair and spins the shuttle ninety degrees to port, so the front of the shuttle is facing the direction it is traveling once again. He plots a return course back to the police cruiser and fires the engines. The shuttle turns to starboard in a large sweeping arc and then straightens out, heading back home to the cruiser.

Nathan walks back to where Carter is laying, falls to his knees, picks him up, pulls him tight and starts to cry. His best friend for almost forty years is dead, taken too early at only forty-four years old. He sits there holding his friend for the next fifteen minutes before gently putting him back on the floor of the shuttle. He is almost back to the cruiser, so he gets up, goes to the front of the shuttle and takes the pilot's seat once again.

Nathan begins his deceleration and when he gets close to the cruiser, the computer's voice says, "Automated landing systems engaged, please release all controls."

Nathan takes his hands off the controls, the shuttle slows down, aligns itself with the rear bay, moves in and touches down in the center of the bay. Nathan shuts down the shuttle's systems and closes the shuttle bay doors.

He activates the comm system and says, "Mr. Black, please report to the shuttle bay and bring a stretcher."

Mr. Black answers a few seconds later, "Aye Captain, I'll be right there."

A few minutes later Mr. Black enters the shuttle bay carrying the stretcher. He approaches and enters the shuttle where he sees Carter's body lying on the floor.

Nathan gets up out of the pilot's seat and says, "Thank you, Mr. Black. If you wouldn't mind helping me carry Carter to the medical bay, we'll put his body in one of the refrigeration units until we can get him home."

"Of course, Captain."

Mr. Black lays the stretcher down beside Carter's body and then he and Nathan lift him and place him on the stretcher. They pick up the stretcher and carry him down to the medical bay where they place him in the refrigeration unit.

Nathan, still wearing his space suit, says, "Thank you, Mr. Black, I'll join you on the bridge after I get out of this suit."

Mr. Black says, "Aye Captain," and leaves the medical bay.

Nathan puts his hand on the glass door of the refrigeration unit next to Carter's head. Tears well up in his eyes as he looks at his best friend's lifeless body lying there, memories of their lives together flashing through Nathan's mind.

After a minute, Nathan heads back to the shuttle bay where he removes his space suit and parks and secures the shuttle in its alcove.

When finished, Nathan heads back up to the bridge whereupon entering he says, “Status report.”

Mr. Nagata who had come up to the bridge from the engine room answers first, “All primary systems are operational, and the force field is holding at the breach. Several of the secondary systems are offline, Captain.”

“Thank you, Mr. Nagata.”

“Ms. Arnoult, any word from Admiral Daniels?”

“Yes, Captain, Admiral Daniels informed me that as a precaution he had already dispatched a battle group to back us up. It should arrive in a little over an hour.”

“Excellent, have you passed that information on to Mr. Tisdale?”

“Yes Captain.”

“Ms. Norata, anything on the sensors?”

“No Captain, the sensors are showing all clear.”

“Good, let’s hope it stays that way until the battle group arrives.”

Tension is high on the bridge, the mood is somber, nobody says anything and the next hour passes slowly.

At an hour and five minutes a warning bell goes off on Ms. Norata’s console and she says, “Captain, there are a dozen EDF ships approaching in FTL from astern.”

Nathan says, “Finally.”

Nathan pushes a button on his chair’s console, so the view screen shows astern. A few moments later, the EDF battle group drops out of FTL about two kilometers away.

All eyes are on the view screen and as the last ship drops out of FTL Nathan stands up and says, “What… the… hell… is… that?”

As the crew scans the view screen, they see five light cruisers, five heavy cruisers, a battle carrier and a ship that unbelievably dwarfs the battle carrier.

Mr. Bell is the first to answer, "I have no idea, Captain, but look at the size of that thing and look at all those laser cannons."

Mr. Black chimes in with, "Holy shit."

Ms. Arnoult interrupts and says, "Captain, we have an incoming transmission from the battle group."

"On screen please, Ms. Arnoult."

"Aye Captain."

The view screen switches to show a high-tech bridge adorned all in white with fluorescent blue highlights. The commanding officer is standing front and center.

"Greetings, Captain Stone. I am Admiral Timothy Anderson, commanding officer of the EDF dreadnought Aurora. We understand you have sustained some battle damage and we're here to pick you up."

"Greetings, Admiral Anderson. Yes, we have a large hull breach on the bridge preventing us from jumping into FTL."

"Very well, Captain Stone, your ship and Mr. Tisdale's transport are cleared for landing in landing bay alpha, port side."

"Thank you, sir."

"You're welcome, Captain. You and your crew are to join me on the bridge after you land."

"Very well, Admiral."

The transmission cuts off and Nathan says, "Ms. Arnoult, tell Mr. Tisdale to follow us into the landing bay."

"Aye Captain."

"Mr. Bell, take us in."

"Aye Captain."

Mr. Bell banks the police cruiser around in a large arc and approaches the dreadnaught from the port side.

Mr. Tisdale manages to turn his transport around and follow them in.

As Nathan's ship gets closer to the dreadnaught, he and his crew are in awe of the sheer size of the ship and the amount of weaponry displayed.

Nathan says, "My God that's a big ship. It looks to be twice the size of a battle carrier."

Mr. Bell lines the ship up with the huge entrance to landing bay alpha. As he gets closer to the dreadnought, he slows the ship down to a slow crawl. Soon the police cruiser passes through the atmospheric force field and into the bay. Once inside, Mr. Bell lowers the landing gear and sets the ship down on the deck. At that point a deckhand steps out in front of the ship with two red flash lights to direct Mr. Bell where to park. Mr. Bell follows his direction into a side bay and then shuts the engines down.

The crew finishes shutting the ship down and then make their way down to the lower bay. They open the ramp and walk down into the Aurora's massive landing bay.

Following them towards the landing bay, Mr. Tisdale engages the automatic landing sequence, giving all control over to the transport's main computer. As it gets closer to the dreadnought, the computer slows the ship down to a slow crawl. Soon the transport passes through the atmospheric force field and into the bay. Once inside, the computer lowers the landing gear and sets the ship down on the deck. The computer then shuts down the engines and all other systems.

Nathan notices two armed Marines, carrying pulse rifles, and a young fleet officer approaching. The fleet officer stops as he reaches the front of Nathan's ship. The two armed Marines continue on over to Mr. Tisdale's transport.

When they reach the rear of the transport, they raise their pulse rifles and one of the Marines says in a raised voice, "Mr. Tisdale would you please open the ramp and exit the transport?"

The fleet officer that stopped at Nathan's ship greets Nathan and his crew by saying, "Welcome aboard the Aurora. I am Lieutenant Green, if you would please follow me, I will escort you to the bridge. Admiral Anderson is waiting for you."

Nathan asks, "What about Mr. Tisdale?"

"He will be detained until the investigation is concluded and he is cleared of all charges against him."

"Very well, Lieutenant, lead on."

Lieutenant Green, Nathan and his crew head off across the huge landing bay. Nathan looks back to see Mr. Tisdale walking down the rear ramp of the transport with his hands on his head and he is taken into custody by the two Marines.

As they walk, Nathan's crew look around and see many ships in the landing bay. There are shuttles, transports, assault craft, cargo pod carriers, fuel tankers, water tankers and even a dozen F-114 Tomcats. There are hundreds of flight crew personnel milling around, working on the ships, fueling them, arming them, and moving them around the bay. The bay is buzzing like a bee hive.

Lieutenant Green leads them over to the internal tram where they board a car and are whisked away at high speed towards the center of the huge dreadnought. When the tram stops, everyone gets off and heads over to a group of elevators.

They all get in an elevator and Lieutenant Green pushes the button for the bridge. The elevator rises at a substantial speed.

After a few seconds Lieutenant Green speaks up and says, "Captain Stone, I wanted to take this opportunity to say it is a real honor to meet you, sir. I studied your tactics and battle records at the academy, and I have to say they are true genius, sir. You're considered a living legend by everyone I know, myself included, sir."

Nathan turns a little red and says, "Thank you, Lieutenant Green, that's very nice of you to say."

"My pleasure, sir."

The elevator reaches the bridge and the doors open. Nathan, his crew and Lieutenant Green step out of the elevator and onto the bridge. Admiral Anderson turns to look at them and walks over to greet them.

Admiral Anderson extends his hand to Nathan and says, "Captain Stone, it is an honor to meet you and welcome aboard the Aurora."

Nathan shakes the admiral's hand and says, "Thank you, Admiral Anderson, it is a pleasure to meet you and thank you for rescuing us."

"My pleasure, Captain Stone. If you and your crew will follow me, please."

The admiral turns and walks to his station at the center of the bridge and says, "Comms, open a channel to the battle group."

"Aye sir, channel open."

"Attention all commands, this is Admiral Anderson on the Aurora. Engage your cloaking devices and sound battle stations. Anderson out."

The admiral presses a button on his command console to close the channel.

"Tactical, engage the cloaking device."

The tactical officer answers, "Aye sir, engaging cloaking device."

Everyone on the bridge watches through the port and starboard side bridge windows as the other ships in the battle group fade out and disappear from view.

A few seconds later the tactical officer says, “Admiral, there is a fleet of ships approaching our position in FTL.”

Admiral Anderson turns and looks at Nathan and says, “Looks like we got here just-in-time, Captain.”

“Yes, it certainly does, Admiral.”

The admiral turns back and says, “XO, sound battle stations.”

“Aye sir.”

The XO grabs the microphone and announces over the ship’s address system, “Battle stations, battle stations, all hands man your battle stations, this is not a drill.”

An alarm sounds after his address and the lights on the bridge change from white to red.

A minute later he says, “Admiral, all sections report battle stations manned and ready.”

“Thank you, XO.”

A few seconds later twenty Xandurian war ships drop out of FTL right in front of the cloaked EDF fleet.

The admiral says, “Funny looking ships, aren’t they? They kind of look like an exotic fish of some type.”

Nathan says, “They certainly are different.”

“Tactical, let’s tag these ships with our new cloaked trackers.”

“Aye sir, firing trackers now.”

A few minutes go by then the tactical officer says, “Admiral, all twenty ships are tagged with the cloaked trackers and all twenty signals are coming in loud and clear. No signs the Xandurians have discovered us, sir.”

A few minutes go by, and then the alien fleet accelerates away rapidly and disappears in bright blue flashes of light as they jump into FTL.

“Tactical, are you still receiving the trackers signals?”

"Aye sir, all twenty trackers are still coming in loud and clear."

"Excellent."

"Comms, open a channel to the battle group."

"Aye sir, channel open."

"Attention all commands, this is Admiral Anderson on the Aurora. Stand down from battle stations, drop your cloaks, come about 180 degrees, set course for Trynx 3 and engage your FTL drives, maximum speed. Anderson out."

The admiral presses a button on his command console to close the channel.

"XO, stand down from battle stations."

"Aye sir."

The XO grabs the microphone and announces over the ship's address system, "All hands, this is the XO. Stand down from battle stations, repeat stand down from battle stations."

An alarm sounds after his address and the lights on the bridge change from red back to white.

"Tactical, disengage the cloaking device."

"Aye sir, disengaging the cloaking device."

"Navigator, plot a course to Trynx 3."

"Aye sir, course plotted and laid in."

"Helm, bring us about 180 degrees."

Shortly thereafter, the Aurora and all the other ships in the battle group start to turn. When they reach the one hundred and eighty degree mark, the other ships accelerate away rapidly and disappear in bright blue flashes of light as they jump into FTL.

The last one to jump is the Aurora.

"Helm, engage the FTL drive and take us up to 14 TSL."

"Aye sir, engaging the FTL drive now."

The ship accelerates rapidly and everyone on the bridge sees a bright blue flash of light through the bridge windows as the ship accelerates past the speed of light.

A little more than a minute later the helmsman says, "Admiral, we have jumped into FTL and have reached 14 TSL. Estimated time to Trynx 3 is one hour."

"Very well Helm, steady as she goes."

"Aye sir."

"XO, you have the bridge."

"Aye sir."

Now that the fleet has safely jumped into FTL and is on its way back to Trynx 3 Admiral Anderson turns his attention back to Nathan and his crew.

He walks over to Nathan, gestures with his right hand towards the elevators and says, "Captain Stone, if you and your crew will follow me, I will show you to our guest quarters so you can freshen up and relax."

"Thank you, Admiral."

Stepping into the elevator Nathan says, "This is quite a ship you have here, Admiral. How did we build such a huge ship in the short time since I left the military? There was no mention of building such a ship when I was an admiral."

"Quite correct, Captain Stone, it was only after the battle with the Sulari that we decided we needed a new, bigger class of ship with more fire power than anything else we have ever built. We knew more battles would be coming, and we wanted even more firepower."

"That battle was a little over a year ago. How did you build this ship so fast?"

"For the first time in Earth's history, we contracted another race to build us a warship, or warships I should say, she has five sister ships."

Nathan's eyes open wide and his jaw drops. "You built six of these in a year?"

"Yes, we contracted the Tyrellians to build them. They have an enormous set of fully automated ship yards that can handle almost any size ship in large numbers. They're quite a technological marvel to behold. The Tyrellians are master ship builders, but even they were a little apprehensive on building ships of this size. At almost twice the size of one of our battle carriers and ten times the fire power, she packs quite a punch."

"And then some, Admiral, and then some."

The elevator arrives on level forty where the guest quarters are located, the doors open and the admiral gestures that everyone should step out with his right hand. Everyone steps out of the elevator and the admiral shows them to their individual quarters, Nathan and Desiree's being the last.

Nathan shakes the admiral's hand and says, "Thank you for the rescue and for the hospitality, Admiral."

"My pleasure, Captain Stone, now you go relax and have a drink. We'll be arriving at Trynx 3 in about an hour. I'll meet you down in the landing bay to see you off."

"Thank you, Admiral."

With that, the admiral turns and heads back to the elevators. Nathan and Desiree step into the guest quarters and the door slides shut behind them. Nathan sees there is a small bar to the left as he walks in and pours himself a full glass of scotch. He parks himself on the couch and takes a large gulp.

Desiree comes over and sits beside him, grabs his hand and looks into his eyes. She can see his pain. He hid it from everyone else, but not from her.

She says, "I'm so sorry about Carter, my love."

Just hearing his name causes Nathan to break down and tears roll down his cheeks. Desiree pulls him close to her and he sobs on her shoulder.

# CHAPTER 4 – BACK TO TRYNX 3

Desiree has spent the last hour trying to console a grief-stricken Nathan. Losing his lifelong best friend Carter has hit him very hard, understandably.

Nathan checks the time and knows they are about to arrive at Trynx 3 so he decides he should head to the washroom to compose himself. As he stands up the Aurora drops out of FTL. Nathan and Desiree see a bright blue flash of light and then the large orange and brown rock that is Trynx 3 appears through the windows in the guest quarters.

Mr. Bell, Mr. Black, Mr. Nagata and Ms. Norata have been relaxing in the adjoining guest quarters and know their arrival at Trynx 3 is their cue to go back to their ship and prep it for takeoff. The four of them meet at the elevators and take one down to the internal tram. They then board a tram and are whisked away at high speed to the landing bay.

Nathan and Desiree leave the guest quarters a minute after the other crew members, so they end up taking a separate elevator and tram. When Nathan and Desiree step off the tram into the landing bay, they look over at their ship and see Admiral Anderson shaking each of the crew member's hands before they walk up the ramp into the ship.

Nathan and Desiree make their way across the bay to their ship and as they approach, the admiral says, "Ah, Captain Stone, I wanted to see you off and let you know it was a pleasure to meet you."

Nathan shakes his hand and says, "It was a pleasure to meet you as well, Admiral, and thank you again for the rescue and for your hospitality. You have an amazing ship here, sir."

"Thank you, Captain Stone, that she is. Safe journey."

The admiral then turns to Desiree, shakes her hand and says, "It was a pleasure to meet you as well. Safe journey."

The admiral turns and walks off across the landing bay heading towards the internal tram.

Nathan and Desiree walk up the ramp into the ship, they close the ramp and head up to the bridge. The rest of the crew are already on the bridge getting the ship ready for takeoff when they enter. Through the bridge windows they see Mr. Tisdale being escorted back into his transport by two armed Marine guards carrying pulse rifles and what they guess is a pilot. They see the ramp close and the transport's engines fire up. After a few minutes, the transport lifts off the deck, turns and heads out the bay doors into space. Shortly after it clears the bay doors, the shuttle dives towards Trynx 3 and disappears from view.

Nathan says, "Okay, people, it's time to go."

"Ms. Arnoult, contact Aurora air traffic control and request clearance for takeoff."

"Aye Captain."

"Mr. Bell, fire up the engines."

"Aye Captain."

The crew hears the jet engines spin up and start.

Shortly after that Ms. Arnoult says, "Captain, Aurora air traffic control has cleared us for takeoff."

"Thank you, Ms. Arnoult."

"Mr. Bell, take her out."

"Aye Captain."

Mr. Bell pushes the throttles forward a little, and the ship begins to rise. When the ship is five feet off the deck, he pulls the landing gear up, rotates the ship one hundred and eighty degrees and then nudges it forward towards the huge bay doors. A few seconds later they pass through the atmospheric force field and out into space.

After they exit the landing bay, Nathan says, "Ms. Arnoult, contact the station and request passage through the defense satellites and then contact air traffic control at the surface compound and request clearance to land."

"Aye Captain."

After a few minutes Desiree says, "Captain, we have clearance through the defense satellites and clearance to land on helipad two in the compound."

"Thank you, Ms. Arnoult."

"Mr. Bell, take us down."

"Aye Captain."

Mr. Bell noses the ship over and begins his approach. They pass through the web of defense satellites and enter the upper atmosphere.

As the ship enters the atmosphere, Nathan looks up at the hull breach above him where he can see the flames of re-entry shooting past. A shiver goes down his spine and the hair on the back of his neck stands up from the mere thought of what would happen if the force field failed at that moment.

He whispers to himself, "I sure hope that force field holds."

Of course, the force field holds, and the flames dissipate as they decelerate. The ship is descending towards the compound from the west. As they approach the compound, Mr. Bell slows the ship down to a crawl and banks the ship to starboard, turning it ninety degrees to line it up with the helipad. Soon the ship is hovering at two hundred feet directly over the helipad. Mr. Bell pulls back on the throttles and the ship descends slowly. When the ship has dropped to fifty feet, the landing gear comes down. A few moments later the wheels touch the ground and Mr. Bell shuts the engines down.

Nathan stands up and says, "Nice smooth landing, Mr. Bell."

"Thank you, Captain."

"All right, everyone, shut everything down and let's go."

The crew finishes shutting down the ship's systems and then they make their way down to the lower bay. They open the ramp and walk out onto the helipad. To their right, over on helipad one, they see Mr. Tisdale being escorted down the ramp of the transport ship by the two Marines.

Desiree asks Nathan, "What do you think will happen to Mr. Tisdale?"

"Oh, I have a feeling he will be just fine. There will be a full investigation, but I am confident when all is said and done, he will be found innocent of any wrong doing and will be set free. After all, his family was held at gun point so what choice did he have? The fact that he stopped and cooperated fully after we informed him that his family had been rescued shows he was acting under duress. If needed I will testify on his behalf and tell the investigative panel exactly that."

Desiree chimes in with a little grin on her face, "And of course the investigative panel will listen to you, how could they disregard the opinion of a 'living legend'?"

Nathan's crew all try not to smile but fail. A couple of them even start to chuckle. All of them cover their mouths with their hands trying to hide their smiles.

Nathan looks at Desiree and says, "I'm never going to live that one down am I?"

A big smile appears on Desiree's face and she says, "Oh, hell no."

Nathan chuckles just a little bit and says, "Okay let's get to work repairing the ship. Mr. Nagata, you're in charge of these.... smartasses. I expect your preliminary assessment in two hours. I'm going to go see Colonel Williamson."

"Aye Captain."

As Nathan walks away, he can hear Mr. Nagata giving the team their orders.

"Mr. Bell, go grab a Tug and let's pull this bird into that hangar so we can assess the damage."

"Mr. Black, head over to the machine shop and see if they have the bulk materials we'll need to make the replacement panels and supports."

"Ms. Norata and Ms. Arnoult, go back up to the bridge and run diagnostics on all the ship's systems. Oh and close the ramp on your way in."

Nathan turns back as he is walking and sees his crew scatter and begin the tasks that Mr. Nagata has assigned them. A smile appears briefly on his face.

Nathan makes his way through the command center to Colonel Williamson's office. He stops at the colonel's aid's desk and asks to see the colonel.

The aid buzzes the colonel and says, "Colonel, Captain Stone is here to see you, sir."

"Excellent, send him in."

"Yes sir. The colonel will see you now, Captain Stone."

"Thank you."

The colonel's door slides open as Nathan approaches it. As Nathan steps into his office, Colonel Williamson stands and walks out from behind his desk.

The two men shake hands and Colonel Williamson says, "Ah, Captain Stone, I want to congratulate you on a job well done intercepting Mr. Tisdale and recovering the ore before the Xandurians got their hands on it."

"Thank you, sir, but I can't take all the credit. It was a team effort. I couldn't have done it without my crew and the officers back on Earth tracking down and rescuing Mr. Tisdale's family."

"I understand you had an altercation with the mystery ship with the bladed energy weapon."

"Yes sir."

"How bad is the damage to your ship?"

"Fairly minor considering, Colonel. The blade cut a large hole in the roof of my bridge. We lost a man before the force field snapped on and sealed the breach."

"I'm so sorry to hear that, Captain, who was it?"

"Captain Carter Rayburn, sir."

"Did you know him well?"

"Yes sir, we were best friends from the age of five."

Nathan chokes up but does his best to stop himself from breaking down in front of the colonel.

The colonel can see the anguish on Nathan's face and the pain in his eyes.

"Oh my God, I'm so sorry, Captain."

"Thank you, sir."

The colonel can tell that Nathan is struggling to keep it together, so he quickly changes the subject.

"Is your crew already beginning the repairs on your ship?"

"Yes sir."

"Well, Captain, I'm sure we have everything needed to complete your repairs and we have the manpower to help you. We have a full staff of aviation mechanics, engineers and machinists here so if you need anything just ask. We'll be more than happy to help."

Both men stand, shake hands and Nathan says, "Thank you very much, Colonel," then Nathan turns to walk out of his office.

Just as Nathan is about to go through the door, the colonel's aid calls on the intercom. "Colonel Williamson, I have Admiral Anderson on the Aurora for you, sir."

Nathan pauses and turns back to look at the colonel.

The colonel waves Nathan back into his office and says, "Put him through."

"Aye sir, putting him through now."

Nathan walks back into the colonel's office as the admiral appears on the video screen on the corner of the desk.

Admiral Anderson says, "Ah, Colonel Williamson, Captain Stone. Good, I'm glad you two are together. I wanted to let you know I asked EDF headquarters for permission to jump to our trackers' location to surveil the Xandurian fleet. I want to see what they are up to. Maybe they will lead me to the base where they are working on their time machine."

Colonel Williamson says, "Best of luck, Admiral. We look forward to your report."

Nathan says, "Yes good luck, Admiral."

"Thank you, gentlemen. Anderson out."

The screen goes back to displaying the EDF logo and Nathan says, "I wish I was going with him, but I have other matters to attend to. If you need me, Colonel, I'm going to go check on my crew and the progress of the repairs."

"Very well, Captain Stone."

Nathan leaves the command center, heads out into the compound and over to the hangar that his cruiser was pulled into. He walks up the ramp into the ship and heads up to the bridge. When he gets there, he sees Mr. Nagata examining the hole in the roof of the bridge.

"Well, Mr. Nagata, what do you think?"

"Well, Captain, I estimate it will take about six days to replace the paneling and supports, repair the damaged systems and run the diagnostics."

"Colonel Williamson told me he has a whole staff of aviation mechanics, engineers and machinists and they are at our disposal."

"That would be excellent, Captain. Could you ask for two mechanics and machinists? They can take care of fabricating the new panels and supports while I concentrate on repairing the damaged systems."

"You got it, Mr. Nagata."

"Thank you, Captain."

Nathan turns to Desiree who is helping Ms. Norata run the diagnostics and says, "Ms. Arnoult, will you please get me Colonel Williamson over in the command center?"

"Aye Captain."

Desiree walks back over to her communications console, puts her headset on and calls over to the command center.

A minute later she says, "Captain, I have Colonel Williamson for you, sir."

"Thank you, Ms. Arnoult, on speakers please."

"Aye Captain, on speakers."

"Colonel Williamson?"

"Yes, Captain Stone, what can I do for you?"

"I'm calling to take you up on your offer of assistance, sir. Can you send over two aviation mechanics and two machinists to assist my engineer with the repairs please?"

"Absolutely, Captain, they are on their way."

"Thank you, Colonel, I appreciate it."

"You're welcome, Captain. Williamson out."

Fifteen minutes later the four men arrive and meet with Mr. Nagata. He instructs them on what he would like them to do.

Together the five of them come up with a plan to get the repairs completed quickly including using the adjustable catwalks in the hangar so they can access the top of the ship a lot easier. The two aviation mechanics climb up and adjust the catwalks so they can walk right over top of the bridge and then they get to work cutting out the damaged panels. Once the damaged outer panels are removed the mechanics move inside the ship to remove the damaged inner panels. At this point the machinists take over, and using a tablet with a built-in laser scanner, they measure for the new supports they will have to fabricate. The machinists take their tablet and the damaged panels back to their machine shop. They then upload the measurements for the supports from the tablet to the main frame. The main frame extrapolates the missing sections to complete the designs for the new supports. After double checking everything, they upload their designs to the milling machine and start it working. Each of the supports will be milled out of a large block of a strong, lightweight titanium alloy to match what was previously used for the skeletal structure of the police cruiser. There are five damaged supports to replace, and each of them will take the better part of a day to mill out. While the first support is being carved out, the machinists work on the replacement panels.

Back on the police cruiser Nathan looks up at the gaping hole in the top of his bridge and says, “I love a convertible as much as the next guy, but this is ridiculous.”

His crew shares a chuckle, shake their heads and then go back to work running diagnostics on all the ships systems to find out which ones were damaged in the attack.

# CHAPTER 5 – ANOTHER LOSS

Six days have passed, and Nathan and his crew have been working diligently on repairing the damaged systems on the police cruiser. Repairs to the ship's systems are almost complete. The machinists finished fabricating the new supports and the new hull panels yesterday. So far today the mechanics have welded in the new supports and have started welding in the new outer hull panels. At the rate they are working the repairs will most likely be completed today.

Come twelve o'clock Nathan realizes he is starving and suggests to the crew they take a break to eat something. Everyone heads down to the galley for lunch. The mood at meal times is much more serious than before, Carter's death still hangs over everything. Nathan is most affected, staying very quiet and serious for the most part which is a big change in his personality. When everyone has finished eating, they head back up to the bridge to continue their repair work. A few minutes after they resume work, the comm system lets out a series of beeps and a green light flashes on Desiree's console.

Desiree says, "Captain, we're being hailed."

"Thank you, Ms. Arnoult, on speakers please."

"Aye Captain."

"This is Captain Nathan Stone."

"Captain Stone, this is Colonel Williamson. I thought you would like to know the Aurora has just dropped out of FTL and Admiral Anderson is about to initiate a video feed."

"Thank you, Colonel, we'll be right there. Stone out."

"Okay everyone, let's head over to the colonel's office and see what Admiral Anderson has found."

Nathan and his crew quickly make their way over to the command center and into the colonel's office. The door is open when they get there, but Nathan knocks on the door jamb to be polite.

“Ah, Captain Stone, please come in. The feed is just coming through now.”

Nathan and his crew walk into the office and gather around the large video screen on the wall to the right of the colonel’s desk.

The colonel’s aid announces over the intercom, “I’m patching the feed from the Aurora through now. Admiral Anderson is broadcasting the feed through to both Trynx 3 and Earth.”

Admiral Anderson appears on the screen standing on the bridge of the Aurora. He starts by saying, “Good afternoon. I won’t bore you all with the minutia of our journey, I will simply show you what we saw when we dropped out of FTL.”

The view changes to show what is displayed on the Aurora’s main view screen. In the center of the screen there is a large asteroid with what appears to be sections of a space station sticking out of it. At the top of the asteroid is what looks like a command center with a communications array. Near the middle of the asteroid appears to be a set of large landing bays with huge bay doors and there are at least a dozen defensive gun turrets visible on this side of the asteroid. Patrolling in a spherical orbit around the asteroid are at least a hundred Xandurian war ships and at least ten squadrons of fighters.

In a hushed tone Nathan says, “Wow, they really want to protect that base and whatever’s inside it. That has to be at least half their fleet.”

Colonel Williamson says, “Indeed, Captain Stone, indeed.”

The view changes back to Admiral Anderson standing on the bridge of the Aurora.

“I’m sure many of you are thinking that the Xandurians are protecting something pretty important in that base. I agree with your assumptions one hundred percent, but I am never one to jump the gun so we will remotely surveil this base in an attempt to ascertain what's inside. We are preparing several cloaked satellites to deploy around the base to keep track of ship movements and we will deploy a series of micro drones inside the base that will allow us to search every square inch of it. I'll update you once we have deployed the satellites and the drones. Anderson out."

After the view screen goes dark Nathan turns to his crew and says, "All right, everyone, back to the ship, we have work to do."

Colonel Williamson looks at Nathan and says, "I'll notify you when Admiral Anderson makes contact again."

"Thank you, Colonel."

Nathan and his crew leave the command center, head out into the compound and back to the hangar to finish up the repairs on the police cruiser.

When they get back to the hangar, one of the aviation mechanics comes over to Nathan and says, "She's all buttoned up, Captain Stone. Just waiting for the paint to dry."

Nathan shakes the mechanic's hand and says, "Thank you, we really appreciate the hard work you and the other men put into the repairs. Please pass my thanks along to the others."

"Will do, Captain Stone, and it was our pleasure, sir."

As the mechanic walks away, Nathan turns to his crew and says, "All right let's get back to work, we still have a few systems to finish repairing before we can run the final diagnostics."

A few hours later Nathan and his crew have just finished the last of the repairs and have begun running the final round of diagnostics when the comm system once again lets out a series of beeps and a green light flashes on Desiree's console.

Desiree says, "Captain, we're being hailed again."

"Thank you, Ms. Arnoult, on speakers please."

"Aye Captain."

"This is Captain Nathan Stone."

"Captain Stone, this is Colonel Williamson. Admiral Anderson has just initiated his video feeds, and I thought you would like to come and take a look."

"Absolutely, Colonel, we'll be right there. Stone out."

"Okay, everyone, let's head back to the colonel's office and see what Admiral Anderson has found."

Nathan and his crew quickly make their way back to the command center and into the colonel's office. When they walk in, they see Colonel Williamson watching the video feeds.

Colonel Williamson looks at Nathan and his crew and says, "Come in, everyone, come in. Admiral Anderson has set up four cloaked satellites and placed them in a circular pattern a few thousand kilometers away from the station."

"Each satellite has multiple cameras so we can see anything and everything around the station. We'll be watching their ship movements and learning their schedules from their feeds."

"The admiral also deployed a small drone that infiltrated the space station's landing bay. The drone in turn released fifty micro drones about the size of a common house fly and they are searching the base room by room to see if we can find out why this base is being so heavily guarded."

Everyone gathers around the large video screen to watch the progress. The screen is segmented up showing multiple video streams. One side of the video screen is split into four quadrants each one displaying a feed from one of the cloaked satellites. These four feeds are showing the base and all the Xandurian warships slowly cruising around. The other side of the screen is split into many small video streams coming from the micro drones that are searching the base.

After a few minutes one of the micro drone streams catches Nathan's eye. He double taps the small image to make it larger. This video feed now covers half the video screen. Everyone watches that stream for a few minutes. They see several uniformed Xandurians holding weapons standing guard around the room and a handful of Xandurians dressed in white coveralls working on what appears to be some sort of machine in the center of the room.

Nathan is the first to speak, "Colonel, could that be a lab full of scientists and if so, could that be the time machine they're building?"

"That would certainly make sense, Captain Stone, and it would explain why they have so many ships guarding the base. Our analysts will watch these streams for a week to determine exactly what is going on inside that base, but if I were a betting man, I would wager you are right, Captain Stone."

The colonel, Nathan and Nathan's crew sit and watch the video feeds from the micro drones for about an hour as the drones infiltrate and map each level of the base.

When the drones have finished mapping the entire base, they take up surveillance positions in key areas such as the command center, the security office, the science lab, the hangar, and all the corridors on those levels so the EDF can learn the Xandurians' personnel schedules.

When all the drones have taken up their surveillance positions Colonel Williamson says, "Now it's up to the analysts back on Earth to gather as much information as they can over the next couple of weeks. Once we have their analysis, we can formulate a plan to destroy the base and the time machine and hopefully put an end to this whole mess."

Nathan says, “In my experience things are never quite that easy, Colonel, but we can always hope I guess. Is Admiral Anderson going to remain at the base?”

“No, Admiral Anderson has already turned the Aurora around and is headed back here to T3. How are the repairs to your ship coming along, Captain?”

“Actually, Colonel, the repairs are complete and we just started the final diagnostics before we came over to your office. If the diagnostic finds nothing wrong, we’ll be heading back to Earth right away.”

The colonel shakes Nathan’s hand and says, “Very well, Captain, have a safe journey home.”

“Thank you, Colonel, and thank you for your hospitality while we were making our repairs.”

The colonel and Nathan nod at each other and then Nathan and his team leave the colonel’s office. They make their way out of the command center, head back across the compound to the hangar and back into their ship.

When they get back, they head up to the bridge to check the diagnostics. The computers couldn’t find anything wrong with any of the systems, so the ship is ready to fly once again.

Nathan says, “Great job team, now let’s prep for takeoff.”

They all answer him back with, “Aye Captain,” and then get to work preparing the ship for takeoff.

Desiree had just taken a seat at the communications console when she received an incoming transmission. “Captain, we have an incoming transmission.”

“On screen please, Ms. Arnoult.”

“Aye Captain.”

The main view screen activates, and the crew sees it is Mr. Tisdale calling.

Nathan says, “Ah, Mr. Tisdale, what can I do for you?”

“Well, Captain Stone, I understand you are heading back to Earth.”

“That’s correct, we’re getting ready for takeoff right now, as a matter of fact.”

“Would it be possible to hitch a ride? The authorities have concluded their investigation and released me just as you thought. I’d like to get off this rock and home to my family as soon as possible, Captain Stone.”

Nathan flashes a slight grin and says, “Of course, Mr. Tisdale, how fast can you pack?”

Mr. Tisdale smiles and says, “Oh, I’m already packed, Captain, I’ll be right out. Thank you, Captain Stone.”

“You’re welcome, Mr. Tisdale. Stone out.”

The main view screen shuts down and Nathan says, “Ms. Norata, would you mind meeting Mr. Tisdale at the ramp and showing him where he can stow his things?”

Ms. Norata turns to walk off the bridge and says, “Not at all, Captain.”

Less than ten minutes later Ms. Norata walks back onto the bridge with Mr. Tisdale in tow.

Nathan stands up to greet Mr. Tisdale, shakes his hand and says, “Welcome aboard, Mr. Tisdale.”

“Thank you, Captain Stone.”

“Ms. Arnoult, contact Trynx 3 air traffic control and request clearance for takeoff.”

“Aye Captain.”

“Mr. Bell, fire up the engines.”

“Aye Captain.”

The crew hears the jet engines spin up and start.

Moments later Desiree says, "Captain, Trynx 3 air traffic control says clearance for vertical takeoff is granted, no traffic in the immediate area."

"Thank you, Ms. Arnoult."

"Mr. Bell, take us up."

"Aye Captain."

Mr. Bell pushes the throttles half way open, and the ship begins to rise. When the ship reaches two hundred feet, he adjusts the thrust vectoring, and the ship starts to move forward. There is no seat for Mr. Tisdale to sit down in, so he is standing behind Nathan's chair holding on to the bulkhead above. Keeping this in mind, Mr. Bell accelerates and climbs more gradually instead of ramming the throttles wide open. Several minutes after takeoff, the sky around the ship turns black as they near the edge of the planet's atmosphere. At this point Mr. Bell disengages the jet engines and closes the air intakes. He then engages the sub-light engines and pushes the throttles up. The ship accelerates and soon achieves escape velocity.

The ship's computer announces in its female voice, "Now leaving Trynx 3's gravity. Artificial gravity plating is coming online."

"Mr. Black, plot a course for Earth."

"Aye Captain, course laid in."

"Mr. Bell, take us home, 14 TSL."

"Aye Captain."

The ship accelerates rapidly away from Earth and soon the crew sees the bright blue flash of light through the bridge windows as the ship enters FTL.

After a few minutes Mr. Bell says, "Captain, we have reached 14 TSL. Estimated time to Earth is approximately six hours."

"Thank you, Mr. Bell. Time to sit back, relax and enjoy the ride."

Moments later a red warning light flashes on both Mr. Bell's and Mr. Black's consoles and an alarm beeps at them in time with the warning lights. They both look down at their consoles to determine what is causing the alarm, but before they can really do anything, the ship violently drops out of FTL and comes to a complete stop. Nathan is thrown out of his chair and tumbles across the floor. Mr. Tisdale is thrown over Nathan's chair, lands in front of it, and then rolls into Nathan. The rest of the crew are thrown against their consoles to which they instinctively grab hold of to stop themselves from being tossed out of their seats.

Nathan stands back up, helps Mr. Tisdale up and says, "What the hell just happened? Why did we stop so suddenly?"

Mr. Black is the first to answer, "I'm not sure yet, Captain. I am starting a sensor sweep of the immediate area."

About thirty seconds later Mr. Nagata comes running onto the bridge, "What the hell just happened? Why did we stop? I just got this damn ship back together. You can't stop like that, it could tear the ship apart."

Nathan says, "Calm down, Mr. Nagata. We didn't stop the ship, the ship stopped itself. We're trying to find out why."

Mr. Black says, "Captain, the sensors are showing a huge debris field directly ahead in our path. The ship detected it and dropped us out of FTL to keep us from flying through it. If it hadn't, we'd all be dead right now."

"What kind of debris, Mr. Black?"

"Sensors show the majority of the debris is metallic with some organic material mixed about. My guess is it was a ship."

Mr. Bell chimes in with, "A damn big ship to leave a debris field this big."

Nathan says, "Agreed. Mr. Black, have the computer analyze the debris and cross check it with known ships in the area. Let's see if we can figure out what ship this was."

"Aye Captain."

A few minutes later Mr. Black says, "Captain, the computer has positively identified the ship as the Terran Trade Federation freighter San Diego. A class one freighter with a crew of one hundred souls."

Mr. Black puts an image of the San Diego on the main viewing screen. Not a pretty ship to be sure, but it was a big ship. The image shows the front of the ship with a sloped nose leading up to the flight deck windows. Behind that is a huge hexagonal box that presumably held the cargo, and behind that was the star drive with a set of very large thrust cones for sub-light travel.

Nathan says, "Wow, she was a big ship. I wonder what took her out? Ms. Arnoult, send a message to Trynx 3 and let them know we discovered the remains of the San Diego and it appears as if all hands were lost."

"Aye Captain."

Ms. Arnoult sends the message to Trynx 3 and then says, "Captain, I have informed Trynx 3 and they are dispatching a battle carrier with a few heavy cruisers to investigate. ETA is about 5 minutes."

"Very well. Thank you, Ms. Arnoult."

Nathan decides to wait until the task force arrives before continuing on to Earth. Two minutes pass and then Ms. Norata's tactical console lights up red and an alarm sounds, warning her that a ship is dropping out of FTL right on top of them.

She's barely able to yell, "CAPTAIN...," before the blade slices into the hull.

The Xandurian ship dropped out of FTL so close to them and was moving so fast that in the blink of an eye the blade weapon had cut the ship in half right through the engineering section. The ship shakes like it's in the middle of a massive earthquake, and the lights flicker on and off several times before the reserve power kicks in. The two pieces of the ship spin out of control and more alarms sound. The ship is depressurizing, so the bridge is experiencing a violent windstorm as the atmosphere vents out into space. Everyone is panicked and screaming in fear. The crew seated at their stations grab onto their consoles. Mr. Nagata and Mr. Tisdale grab onto a chair and a console to keep from getting sucked out of the bridge. The door to the bridge finally slides shut, stopping the windstorm.

Nobody can believe what just happened. As the front of the ship spins around the crew sees the Xandurian ship with the bladed energy weapon extended down from its nose cruising away.

Mr. Nagata quickly checks the reactor's status on his engineering console and yells, "CAPTAIN, THE REACTOR IS ABOUT TO BREACH! WE NEED TO GET OUT OF HERE NOW!"

"MR. BELL, LAUNCH THE LIFEBOAT!"

"AYE CAPTAIN!"

"MS. ARNOULT, BROADCAST A MAYDAY WITH OUR POSITION!"

"AYE CAPTAIN!"

Mr. Bell opens a small door at the top of his console slams his fist down on a big red button. This sets off a whole series of explosive bolts immediately behind the bridge door which cut through the hull, separating the front section of the ship from the front half of the engineering section. A small set of maneuvering thrusters kicks in and pushes the lifeboat away from the rest of the ship. Mr. Bell vectors the lifeboat away so he can put as much distance between them and the doomed engineering section as he can before the reactor goes critical.

Nathan looks out the port side bridge windows and sees the Xandurian ship is coming about and heading towards the lifeboat with the blade weapon still deployed.

"I think they mean to finish us off."

The Xandurian ship has slowed, but it is getting closer and closer to the lifeboat.

Mr. Nagata interrupts, "The reactor is going critical."

A few seconds later they see a bright white flash from behind them as the reactor explodes with the force of a high yield nuclear warhead.

The Xandurian ship is now only fifty meters away and closing. A few seconds before the bladed energy weapon makes contact with the hull, the shock wave from the reactor explosion hits and pushes the lifeboat clear of the blade. Nathan looks out the starboard bridge windows and sees the Xandurian ship coming about to take another run at them. The Xandurian ship completes its turn and heads straight for the lifeboat when once again Ms. Norata's tactical console lights up red and an alarm sounds. She looks down to see that five EDF ships are approaching their position in FTL. The ships drop out of FTL right behind the lifeboat.

Ms. Norata says, "Oh thank heaven, it's the Invincible and her escorts."

A few seconds later the Xandurian ship is rocked by a number of large explosions as the Invincible and the four heavy cruisers open fire with their massive laser cannons and pummel the Xandurian ship. The Xandurian's shields don't last long under the intense barrage from the EDF capital ships. After the shields fail, pieces of the ship are being blown off. The Xandurian ship is taking quite a beating. It's massively out gunned so it vectors away, accelerates rapidly and jumps into FTL before the Invincible and her escorts can finish her off. From what Nathan and his crew could tell the Xandurian ship took massive damage before it escaped.

Just then Desiree says, "Captain, we are being hailed."

"Thank you, Ms. Arnoult, on speakers please."

"Aye Captain."

Over the speakers comes, "Attention survivors on the lifeboat, this is Admiral Jameson on the Invincible. We're preparing to bring your lifeboat aboard. Please acknowledge."

"Admiral Jameson, this is Captain Stone, are we ever glad to see you, sir. My whole crew survived unharmed and we will sit tight and wait to be brought aboard."

"Acknowledged, Captain Stone, and I'm glad that everyone is okay. See you shortly. Jameson out."

Nathan, his crew and Mr. Tisdale gather around the port side bridge windows and watch as the massive battle carrier slowly pulls alongside their tiny lifeboat.

When the lifeboat is amid ship and lined up with one of the port side landing bays, a tractor beam powers up, grabs hold of the lifeboat, and pulls it into the bay. Before long the lifeboat is passing through the shuttle bay's atmospheric force field and is gently set down on the deck.

Mr. Nagata walks to the rear of the bridge and pushes a series of buttons on the control pad beside the door. The door slides open, everyone exits the lifeboat, and they are greeted by a full ground crew and two medics. The medics check with everyone to make sure they are okay.

Admiral Jameson comes walking over, shakes Nathan's hand and says, "Captain Stone, I'm glad you and your people are all okay."

"Yes, thank you, Admiral, you showed up just in the nick of time."

The admiral says, "You're welcome, Captain Stone."

The admiral gestures to a Marine guard standing nearby and says, "The corporal will show you to the guest quarters. We'll give you a lift home to Earth, while the rest of the task force stays here to search for survivors from the freighter."

"Thank you, Admiral."

The admiral turns, walks away and says, "No problem, Captain Stone."

Nathan, his crew and Mr. Tisdale follow the Marine across the landing bay to the internal tram. The tram takes them to the elevators near the center of the ship. They take an elevator up to level forty to the guest quarters where they are each shown into their own private state room.

After entering their room, Nathan goes over to the huge windows which overlook the flight deck. The battle carrier accelerates rapidly, and Nathan and Desiree see a bright blue flash of light through the windows as the ship accelerates past the speed of light.

Suddenly Nathan just drops into one of the chairs facing the windows. He puts his face in his hands and yells, "SON OF A BITCH!"

Desiree comes running over, kneels down beside him, and puts her arm around Nathan's shoulders.

She asks him, "What's wrong, sweetheart?"

Nathan sits quietly with his face still in his hands for a few seconds, then he slowly raises his face out of his hands. Desiree can see tears in his eyes and running down his cheeks.

Desiree repeats, "What's wrong, sweetheart?"

Nathan replies quietly, "We forgot Carter. His body was in the medical bay in one of the refrigeration units."

Desiree hugs him and says, "Oh my God, honey, you can't blame yourself for that. The attack was so sudden we barely got out in time."

"I know, but now I can't even bury my best friend. He's just gone."

"Let me pour you a drink, you could use one."

Desiree goes over to the bar and pours Nathan a large scotch, brings it over to him, sits down beside him, and they sit and watch the stars go by for hours.

Almost six hours later the Invincible arrives back at Earth. In their respective guest quarters Nathan, his crew and Mr. Tisdale see a bright blue flash of light through the windows as the ship drops out of FTL and then the Earth suddenly appears in front of the massive battle carrier.

Everyone comes out of their guest quarters and meet up at the elevators. They take an elevator down to the internal tram which they take back to the landing bay.

When they arrive in the landing bay, they see there is a shuttle waiting to take them down to the planet. They board the shuttle and take their seats.

A few minutes later the pilot comes out of the cockpit and asks Nathan, "Is this everyone, sir?"

"Yes, we're all here."

"Very well, sir, we'll be lifting off in just a few minutes."

The pilot goes back into the cockpit and begins his launch sequence. The side door closes, and the engines start up.

A few minutes later everyone hears the engines power up and then the shuttle lifts off the deck. When it's about five feet off the deck, it turns ninety degrees and starts to move forward towards the huge shuttle bay doors.

Looking out the side windows, everyone watches as the shuttle passes through the atmospheric force field and out into space. Immediately after they clear the edge of the shuttle bay, the ship dives straight down towards the planet.

This sharp maneuver doesn't bother Nathan and his crew as they are used to those kinds of forces being exerted on their bodies. Mr. Tisdale however, is not used to them and he is doing his best to fight the urge to throw up. The shuttle is taking them down to the Planetary Police headquarters in Seattle. They come in over the ocean and land on the helipad where they see Mrs. Tisdale and the Tisdale's two children are waiting for them.

The pilot shuts the engines down and opens the side door of the shuttle. When Mr. Tisdale exits the shuttle, he runs to his wife and kids and hugs all three of them at the same time. He then kisses his wife and tells her he loves her.

Nathan and his crew exit the shuttle and walk over to the Tisdales. Mr. Tisdale introduces his wife and kids to everyone.

After the introductions, Mrs. Tisdale says, "I wanted to thank you all for helping rescue me and my children from those horrible aliens and for bringing John home to us."

She then walks over to Nathan and looks into his eyes. She sees the pain behind them, so she takes his hands in hers and says, "I am so very sorry to hear you lost someone very special to you while you were trying to save my husband. You have my deepest sympathies and my undying gratitude."

Nathan cannot speak. With tears in his eyes he squeezes her hands a little tighter, gives her a little smile and nods his head to say, "You're welcome."

Mr. Tisdale says, "Yes, thank you all for what you have done," then he looks at Nathan, "and for what you have sacrificed for us."

Nathan's team acknowledges what the Tisdale's have said in the same manner that Nathan did, with a little smile and a nod.

The Tisdale's both say, "Take care, all of you." They then turn, walk over to a waiting car and get in. The car drives off, turns onto the street in front of the police headquarters and is soon out of sight.

After composing himself Nathan turns to his crew and says, "Okay, everyone, the chief wants to see us, better not keep him waiting."

They head into the building and take the elevator up to the top floor. When they exit the elevator, the chief's assistant is waiting for them. He guides them right into the chief's office. As they enter his office, the chief stands up and walks around his desk to greet them.

First, he shakes Nathan's hand and says, "Welcome back, Captain Stone. I am so sorry about Captain Rayburn, I know you two were like brothers."

"Thank you, sir."

The chief then addresses them all, "Welcome back, all of you. I'm so happy you made it home safe and sound. Now that you are home, I want you all to get the heck out of here. I'm giving you all two weeks off paid bereavement leave. Captain Stone, if at the end of the two weeks you need more time, just let me know."

"Thank you, sir. Can you assign someone to ferry us home, sir?"

"No need, Captain Stone, you can take your ship."

"Uh, our ship was destroyed, sir."

"Yes, I realize that, Captain Stone, you can take your new ship." The chief walks over to the windows in his office and motions for everyone to come and take a look.

The team moves over to the windows, looks down and sees what appears to be a sleek black and white police cruiser being towed over to the helipad.

Nathan looks down at the ship and then back at the chief with a puzzled look on his face.

The chief looks at Nathan and says, "It was Captain Rayburn's cruiser. I think he would want you to have it, don't you?"

Nathan just smiles and nods his head then turns and shakes the chief's hand. "Thank you, sir, I'll be in touch."

Nathan and his crew turn and walk out of the chief's office. They make their way out to the elevators and head down to the ground floor. Upon exiting the building, they see their new ship sitting on the helipad. It is a very sleek looking, high tech craft that appears to be a bit bigger than their old ship. Nathan wonders if it will fit in his hangar back in Jasper as the tails look quite a bit taller than the old ship.

As they approach the ship a member of the ground crew walks towards them.

When they meet, the man holds his hand out to Nathan and says, "Captain Stone? I'm Crew Chief Oliver."

Nathan shakes his hand and says, "It's a pleasure to meet you, Chief Oliver."

"I'm here to handover your new cruiser."

Reaching into his pocket, he pulls out a few nano-storage disks, hands one to each crew member and says, "Here are the operations manuals. I know you have your own engineer, I will make myself available to him should he have any questions."

"Thank you, Chief Oliver."

Nathan motions to Mr. Nagata to step forward, "This is my engineer, Mr. Nagata. Why don't you two take a few minutes so you can discuss anything he absolutely needs to know before we take this thing for a first flight?"

Mr. Nagata steps up, shakes his hand and says, "It's a pleasure to meet you, Chief Oliver."

"It's a pleasure to meet you as well, Mr. Nagata."

The two walk off across the helipad and around the ship. The crew sees Chief Oliver pointing to various parts of the ship as they walk.

Nathan turns to the rest of his crew and says, “Well, should we go in and check her out?”

The other members of the crew all answer with a resounding, “Aye Captain.”

The new ship has a lower ramp very similar to the old ship, so they walk up the ramp and head inside. Everyone heads up to the bridge and are pretty impressed with what they see. Along the way they can’t help but notice that everything is finished in a glossy white polycarbonate material, except for the floor which seems to be a black rubberized mat. They also notice the ship is amazingly clean like it was brand new, never used.

As they enter the bridge, they notice that almost entire bridge is finished in the same gloss white polycarbonate. The walls, the support beams, the roof, even the floor is made of the same gloss white material though it is coated with a non-slip material. All the consoles and chairs are sleek gloss white polycarbonate with molded curves everywhere and all the touch screen displays are finished in gloss black with all the control interfaces displayed in a medium blue that glows just slightly.

All the lighting in the bridge is hidden and recessed, with the majority of the lighting being bright white, there are blue ribbons of light encircling the base of every console and chair on the bridge.

Nathan is the first to comment, “Wow, that’s a lot of white. A little too much for me. It’s too bright and too clean. I knew Carter was a neat freak, but this is way over the top.”

Desiree chimes in with, “Yeah, it’s a bit too much.”

Mr. Bell says, “The consoles are just too cool though.”

Mr. Black says, “This is amazing.”

Ms. Norata says, "It is pretty bright, but that's a minor concern. Let me at the weapons console so I can see how bad this ship really is."

The crew chuckles at her comment.

Nathan is the first to step onto the bridge almost afraid that he will leave dirty footprints on the pristine floor.

As he steps in a voice comes out of nowhere and says, "Recognize, Nathan Stone, Captain, Earth's Planetary Police Force. Welcome aboard, Captain Stone."

Nathan is startled by the voice then asks, "Who is speaking?"

"I am Vanessa, the ship's artificial intelligence computer interface. I am a fully interactive control system for every system on board this ship."

Nathan and his crew are impressed once again and look at each other with smiles on their faces as if to say, "Now that is just plain cool."

Nathan asks, "Who named you Vanessa?"

"Captain Rayburn did. I was originally programmed to respond to the term 'Computer', but Captain Rayburn felt that was impersonal, so he changed my programming to respond to Vanessa. I was sorry to hear about Captain Rayburn's death."

Nathan laughs a little, shakes his head and wipes a few tears from his eyes.

Desiree steps into the bridge to ask Nathan what's wrong, but Vanessa interrupts her, "Recognize, Desiree Arnoult, Lieutenant, Earth's Planetary Police Force. Welcome aboard, Lieutenant Arnoult."

Once Vanessa has finished speaking Desiree asks Nathan, "What's wrong sweetheart? What's the significance of the name Vanessa?"

"About ten years ago Carter was engaged to a woman he said was the love of his life. She was beautiful and kind and he loved her with all his heart and soul. Two days before they were supposed to get married, they were eating breakfast together, everything seemed okay. She got up from the kitchen table and collapsed on the floor. She suffered some sort of brain aneurism and died in his arms before the paramedics could get there. As far as I know he was never with another woman. Her name was Vanessa. It would be just like him to name the ship's computer Vanessa. Maybe in his mind he was talking to her again."

At that point Nathan looked at Desiree and the other crew members and saw they all had tears in their eyes.

Once again, he composes himself and says, "Well, we better get on with it."

The rest of the crew enters the bridge and Vanessa greets each of them the same way. The crew goes about their duties checking out the systems of this new ship. They even interact with Vanessa a little, asking her questions here and there.

After about an hour, Mr. Nagata walks onto the bridge. When Vanessa greets him the same way she greeted the other members of the crew, she startles him enough that he loses his balance and falls backwards while cursing in Japanese. The rest of the crew burst out in laughter.

Mr. Nagata gets back up and asks, "What the hell was that?"

Nathan says, "That is Vanessa, the ship's artificial intelligence. Go ahead say hello."

Mr. Nagata tilts his head, looks up at the roof and says, "Hello, Vanessa."

"Hello, Engineer Nagata."

Mr. Nagata's face goes blank, and he turns around and walks off the bridge without saying another word.

Nathan chuckles and then turns to ask Mr. Bell, "Well, have you figured out how to fly this thing yet?"

Mr. Bell turns and says, "Captain, I can fly anything, but right now I'm afraid I might scratch this thing."

Vanessa chimes in and asks, "Lieutenant Bell, would you like me to fly for now until you are more familiar with my controls?"

Mr. Bell looks at Nathan as if to say, "What do you think?"

Nathan shrugs and says, "Sure, why not?"

Vanessa says, "Very well. Destination?"

Mr. Black says, "Jasper, Alberta, Canada. I'm entering the exact coordinates now."

"Coordinates received. Course laid in. Preparing for takeoff."

The lower ramp begins to close, and the crew hears the engines spin up and start.

Vanessa says, "I have contacted Seattle air traffic control and received clearance for a vertical takeoff. Prepare for takeoff."

The engines wind up to full power, the ship lifts off and rises straight up until they are at one thousand feet. The ship then starts to move forward and bank to port in a long slow arc. When the ship is pointed in the right direction, it accelerates to five hundred knots and climbs to thirty thousand feet. Once there, the ship levels out and cruises along smoothly.

Vanessa says, "We have reached our cruising altitude of thirty thousand feet. We should arrive in Jasper in approximately one hour and fifteen minutes."

Nathan says, "Very well, Vanessa, nicely done."

"Thank you, Captain Stone."

The crew spends the next hour going over the ship's systems and they share some of their findings with each other. This ship is very similar in many ways to their old ship. It's fast, armed to the teeth, has a cloaking device, and is stuffed full of the latest technology.

After about an hour Vanessa says, “Beginning our descent into Jasper. I have contacted Jasper air traffic control and received an approach vector and clearance for a vertical landing at the specified coordinates.”

As they approach Nathan’s home in Jasper, Vanessa slows the ship down to a crawl and lines it up with the helipad. Soon the ship is hovering at two hundred feet directly over the helipad. Vanessa reduces power, and the ship descends slowly. When the ship has dropped to fifty feet, the landing gear comes down. A few moments later the wheels touch the ground and Vanessa shuts the engines down.

Nathan says, “Nicely done, Vanessa.”

“Thank you, Captain Stone.”

The team exits the ship and they go into the house to get settled in. Nathan grabs the Tug and backs the new ship into his hangar. The higher tails just clear the hangar door. Nathan secures the ship and the hangar for the night and then heads back into the house.

Over the next two weeks the team spends time relaxing and some time getting to know their new ship. Nathan is very quiet and withdrawn, spending a lot of his down time sitting alone on his deck staring at the mountains while sipping on a good single malt scotch. He also spends time driving a few of his antique muscle cars through the mountains. Everyone deals with loss in different ways, this is how Nathan grieves. Even so, Desiree and the rest of his crew are worried about him.

# CHAPTER 6 – SPECIAL FORCES

While Nathan and his crew are on leave, the EDF analysts are busy learning all they can about the Xandurian base where the time machine is being built. The analysts sit for two weeks straight watching the video streams from the cloaked satellites deployed around the station and the fly sized drones inside the station. While watching these video streams, the analysts make notes about certain events and document the Xandurians' patterns of behavior. Everything is about schedules. They learn everything they can about their fleet movements, supply shipments, and fighter patrol schedules. The analysts also document the scientists' schedule and the guards' schedule inside the station. They also analyze the station itself for strengths, weaknesses and defensive capabilities.

When they feel they have collected enough data, they enter everything they have found into a supercomputer for its recommendation on what type of attack to launch and the timing of the attack for the highest probability of success while minimizing human casualties. The super computer chews on all the supplied information for days analyzing every type of attack that the EDF is capable of launching against the Xandurian base.

The super computer rules out any kind of brute force attack by the EDF fleet. The asteroid surrounding the base is just too big, and the base is just too fortified to guarantee the destruction of the time machine, the lab it's in, and the base computer system that houses all the data on the time machine. It also wouldn't guarantee that all the scientists working on the time machine would be eliminated.

The super computer recommends a stealth attack by covertly inserting two special forces teams to destroy the time machine, destroy the base computer core and eliminate all the scientists. It calculates that such a mission has about a seventy-eight percent chance of success with minimal casualties.

This information is given to the powers that be in both the EDF and Earth's world government. After minimal debate the operation is green lighted, and preparation begins.

The Xandurian time machine is determined to be a major threat to not only Earth's security, but to the entire galaxy and the current timeline. It needs to be taken out as soon as possible.

The EDF assigns their two top special forces teams to the mission. All video feeds and previously captured data is provided to the teams so they can begin preparations for the mission. The teams start by studying their insertion point, the base's hangar.

Using the drone surveillance footage, they map out the hangar, scan for security surveillance systems, record security guard patterns, record their shift changes and record the arrival and departure schedules for any ships over the last two-week period.

Fleet Admiral Timothy Daniels has personally taken charge of this operation. He has been informed that the leaders of the two special forces teams have already discovered a problem with the plan, so he is heading to the base where the teams are performing their analysis and preparing for the mission. When his transport lands at the base, Admiral Daniels is directed to the teams' tactical training building and then escorted into the tactical analysis center where he finds the two team leaders going over the video footage of the hangar.

When Admiral Daniels enters the room, one of the team leaders sees him and immediately yells, "ATTENTION ON DECK!" After which both of the team leaders snap to attention and salute him.

Admiral Daniels returns their salute and says, "At ease, gentlemen."

All three men sit down at the large video analysis station at the front of the room.

The admiral says, “I understand you have hit a snag with this plan, so I thought I would stop by and see if we can’t work through it together.”

The first team lead, Lieutenant Jason Stephens says, “Yes, sir, we have discovered that the hangar security systems include an infrared scanner we think will see the heat signature of our cloaked transport when we land in the hangar. As I’m sure the admiral is well aware, our cloaking devices bend light around our ships to hide them but can’t mask the heat from our engines.”

Admiral Daniels answers, “Yes, of course, Lieutenant.” He pauses for a few seconds and then says, “What if I told you that you don’t have to worry about sneaking a cloaked ship into the base’s hangar?”

The second team lead, Lieutenant Robert Grayson asks, “What do you mean, Admiral? How do we sneak into the hangar without a cloaked ship?”

“When I was put in charge of this mission, I had my people go through every database on the planet to find anything we could on the Xandurians.”

“One thing we found was a few weeks back, Captain Nathan Stone of Earth’s Planetary Police, was sent to Solaris 5 to arrest and remove an alien that was running amuck in several of the resorts.”

“Turns out that alien was a Xandurian. Captain Stone had no choice but to put the Xandurian down after which he transported the body back to Earth on his police cruiser.”

“After reading the report I thought the Xandurian had to get to Solaris 5 somehow. On a hunch I sent one of our light cruisers to Solaris 5 to see if they could locate his ship.”

“Indeed, it was there, so we took possession of it and transported it up to the cruiser. It’s en route now and is scheduled to arrive around twenty-one hundred hours tonight."

Lieutenant Stephens smiles and says, "Well that solves that problem doesn't it?"

The admiral gets up and walks towards the door, "Don't celebrate too soon. Someone still needs to learn how to fly it."

The admiral opens the door and two corporals walk in carrying two large metal suitcases. They put the suitcases down on the table and open them up to reveal what appear to be twenty sets of metallic armbands with electronic touch pad control interfaces.

Lieutenant Grayson stands and asks, "What do we have here, Admiral?"

"Oh these? These are the solution to your next problem. Next generation, wearable, personal holographic projectors that will make you appear to be Xandurians. These will allow you to waltz right into the Xandurian base without setting off any alarms."

As the admiral and the two corporals exit the room, the admiral yells back, "Let me know if you run into any more snags."

Lieutenant Grayson looks at Lieutenant Stephens and says, "Very cool. I can't wait to try these babies out."

"Yeah well we have lots of work left to do so put those things away and let's get back to it."

Lieutenant Grayson says, "Roger that," and then closes the suitcases.

In another part of the building, in the middle of a very large hangar, the rest of the team is finishing up the construction of a mockup of the Xandurian base's science lab and the computer core. They will use the mockups combined with the video surveillance streams to layout their attack and work on their timing to maximize their chance at success.

Over the course of the next two weeks, the special forces teams finalize their plan of attack and then run simulation after simulation, making adjustments with each run through until the team leaders are satisfied that they have better than a ninety-five percent chance of successfully completing their mission.

Lieutenant Stephens' team has been tasked with destroying the time machine and eliminating the scientists. Lieutenant Grayson's team has been tasked with destroying the base's computer core which will hopefully wipe out all the research data regarding the time machine.

After running through the simulations hundreds of times, they have the timing of every step down to the second and their teams could literally run the operation in their sleep.

Meanwhile on the other side of the base, the EDF fleet's best pilot, Lieutenant Marcus Hamersley, has been working with a crew of flight engineers to figure out how to fly the Xandurian ship recovered from Solaris 5. Not the easiest task in the world, trying to figure out the flight controls of an alien spacecraft when you can't read or speak their language. There was a lot of trial and error to figure out what button did what, how to control the ship and how the ship reacts to pilot input, but after two weeks Lieutenant Hamersley can fly the ship well enough to fly it out of the landing bay on a dreadnought, make a short FTL jump to the Xandurian base, and then land it in the base's landing bay.

The two special forces teams and Lieutenant Hamersley are as ready as they ever will be. Lieutenant Stephens and Lieutenant Grayson load their teams onto two transports and head for orbit to rendezvous with an EDF light cruiser. Lieutenant Hamersley boards the Xandurian ship and follows the two transports up to the cruiser. When the teams' transports and the Xandurian ship are safely aboard, the cruiser leaves Earth's orbit, jumps into FTL and begins its six-hour journey to Trynx 3.

When the cruiser arrives at Trynx 3, the two special forces teams board their transports again. Lieutenant Hamersley boards the Xandurian ship and then all three ships leave the cruiser and transfer over to the Aurora. It was decided that the mission's best chance of success was to send a lone ship to avoid detection, but that lone ship should be able to defend itself against a large number of enemy ships. A dreadnought is most certainly capable of doing that.

Shortly after the three ships set down in the Aurora's landing bay, the massive dreadnought breaks out of Trynx 3's orbit and jumps into FTL to begin its six-day journey to the Xandurian base.

After six uneventful days, the Aurora activates its cloaking device and drops out of FTL when they are approximately two hours away from the Xandurian base.

Lieutenant Stephens and Lieutenant Grayson lead their teams back down to the landing bay where Lieutenant Hamersley is already getting the Xandurian ship ready to launch.

Admiral Anderson meets them in the bay to wish them luck and shakes each team members' hand before they board the ship.

When everybody is aboard, Lieutenant Hamersley fires up the engines, lifts off the deck, and turns one hundred and eighty degrees. He nudges the ship forward and a few seconds later they pass through the landing bay's atmospheric force field and out into space. Once outside he makes a ninety-degree turn to port and jumps into FTL.

Back on Earth, Nathan and his team have been back at work for a few weeks. For the most part everything is back to normal, though Nathan is not quite back to his cheerful self.

The team has been working on a minor case local to the Seattle area. They are reviewing a bunch of surveillance videos pertaining to their case when the police chief walks in.

The chief says, “Good morning, all.”

Nathan and his team stand and greet the chief, “Good morning, Chief.”

“Captain Stone, I just got a call from Admiral Daniels over at EDF headquarters. His strike teams are about to arrive at the Xandurian station where the time machine is suspected of being developed.”

“He knows how much you and your team have invested in this operation, so he has extended an invitation for us to watch the live video streams from EDF headquarters. If you and your team are interested in joining me, we’ll leave in five minutes.”

Nathan and the others all smile and Nathan answers, “Absolutely, Chief.”

“Very well, Captain Stone. You and your team meet me in the underground parking area in five minutes.”

“Yes sir.”

Nathan turns to his team and says, “You heard the chief, meet in the underground parking area in five minutes.”

Everyone answers, “Aye Captain.”

The chief turns, exits the room, heads back to his office to grab a few things and then heads to the elevators. Nathan and his team disperse out of the room shortly after the chief, quickly grab their things and go to the elevators. They take the elevator down to the basement level and walk out into the secure underground parking area where they see the chief standing next to two police cars.

“Hop in, everyone, let’s go.”

Nathan jumps in the driver's seat of the first car, Chief Tanner sits in the front passenger seat and Mr. Bell and Ms. Arnoult sit in the rear passenger seats.

Mr. Black jumps in the driver's seat of the second car, Mr. Nagata sits in the front passenger seat and Ms. Norata sits in one of the rear passenger seats.

Nathan and Mr. Black put the cars in gear, step on the gas and drive up the ramp to street level.

As they are turning onto the street in front of police headquarters, the chief says to Nathan, "Better hit the lights and sirens and step on it. We don't want to miss anything."

Nathan says, "Yes sir."

He then turns on the lights and sirens, slams the accelerator down on the floor and the police car launches like a race car.

When Mr. Black sees Nathan's car take off at high speed, he smiles, turns on the lights and sirens, and slams the accelerator down on the floor.

Mr. Black says, "Better hold on to something."

Everyone in the car grabs on as the car accelerates rapidly.

EDF headquarters is only about fifteen minutes away from police headquarters. Nathan and Mr. Black are pretty sure they set a new record time for that drive this morning, arriving in just about eleven minutes.

When they arrive at EDF headquarters, they park the police cars out front and walk over to the front doors of the building.

They are met by a young female lieutenant who says, "Good morning, everyone. If you will follow me, I will take you to the command center where Admiral Daniels is waiting for you."

Chief Tanner says, "Lead the way."

They follow her into the building, through security and then over to the elevators. They take an elevator up to the top floor where the young lieutenant guides them through the security scanners and into the command center.

Admiral Daniels comes over to greet them, shakes the chief's and Nathan's hands and says, "Perfect timing, the teams are just a few minutes out. Please have a seat and the video feeds will be patched through shortly."

As they sit down the wall of video screens light up as the video streams initiate. They can see the streams from the cloaked satellites, the streams from the drones inside the base, the streams from the commandeered Xandurian ship and the streams from the body cameras that the special forces teams are wearing. There is a lot of information coming at them all at once.

They can also hear the audio coming in from the special forces teams on the commandeered Xandurian ship. They hear Lieutenant Hamersley say, "Okay men gear up. We'll be dropping out of FTL in one minute."

The members of the special forces teams power up their pulse rifles and engage their personal hologram devices, after which they all appear to change into Xandurian soldiers.

Nathan and everyone else in the command center can hear the team leaders giving last-minute instructions to their teams, "Okay gentlemen, just like we practiced it, by the numbers. Stay focused and keep your cool in there."

Lieutenant Hamersley says, "Dropping out of FTL in 3... 2... 1... now."

In an instant, the commandeered Xandurian ship shows on the video feeds from the cloaked satellites. At the same time the Xandurian base and a bunch of Xandurian ships show on the video feed from commandeered Xandurian ship.

As soon as they drop out of FTL, they are contacted by the base's air traffic control. Lieutenant Hamersley engages his translator and hears he is being asked about his destination and what he is carrying. He answers back, through the translator, that he is bound for the base's landing bay, and that he is carrying a security detail for the scheduled shift change. After a few seconds he hears back that he has clearance to land.

Having observed the activity at the Xandurian base for weeks now, a definite schedule was laid out and it was decided that the special forces teams would go in as replacement security forces. The Xandurians didn't seem to care that the ship carrying the security shift change has arrived an hour early today.

The various video streams show the large landing bay doors open on the Xandurian base. Everyone watches as Lieutenant Hamersley lines up his approach, slows the ship down, and sets it down gently in the right side of the landing bay, exactly how the Xandurians have been doing it for the past few weeks. After the ship sets down, the large landing bay doors close. Lieutenant Hamersley lowers the loading ramp on the ship and the special forces teams, who look like Xandurians thanks to their personal holographic projectors, file out into the bay where they line up exactly as the Xandurians would.

When they are ready, they march in formation over to the entrance to the main corridor that connects the landing bay with the rest of the base.

Upon entering the corridor, alpha team turns right and heads for the science lab containing the time machine. Beta team turns left and heads towards the central computer core.

Along the way, both teams pass groups of Xandurians in the corridors. Their heart rates and blood pressure are way up, and everyone holds their breath as they pass each group of Xandurians, praying that the holographic projectors work to conceal their true identities.

The science lab is four levels above the landing bay, so the ten men of alpha team, led by Lieutenant Stephens, march into one of the elevators and head up to the lab.

The central computer core is six levels down from the landing bay, so the ten men in beta team, led by Lieutenant Grayson, march into one of the elevators and head down to the core.

When the elevators reach their respective floors, Lieutenants Stephens and Grayson are the first to step out of the elevators. Each are greeted by two Xandurian soldiers standing guard. Just as they observed on the video streams there are no words exchanged at all, just simple salutes.

The teams exit their respective elevators and the Xandurian soldiers enter the elevators to leave just as they always do. Why wouldn't they? They've just been relieved the same way as any other day. None of them noticed that they were being relieved an hour early.

Each team leaves two men at the elevators, mimicking the Xandurians exactly. The remaining eight men of each team head to the science lab and the computer core.

When Lieutenant Stephens and his team reach the science lab, he enters the code to open the lab door (acquired by moving one of the fly size drones close to the keypad) and the team enters.

Each member of his team replaces one of the Xandurian guards in the same manner as at the elevator. No words are spoken, just a simple salute.

After the last real Xandurian guard leaves the science lab, and the door closes behind them, Lieutenant Stephens activates his radio and whispers, "Alpha team leader to beta team leader. We are in the lab and are about to start placing the charges."

Alpha team is not alone in the science lab. The scientists working on the time machine are in there with them, so they have to be careful not to draw attention to themselves when placing the explosive charges.

There are computer consoles all around the lab and the time machine. Each member of the team is standing just in front of a console. So as not to be noticed, they all slowly back up until they bump into the work ledge of the computer consoles. Each man takes an explosive charge in his hand, puts his hand behind his back, and sticks the charge to the bottom of the work ledge.

Eleven levels below, Lieutenant Grayson's team enters the computer core and replaces the real Xandurian guards.

Lieutenant Grayson activates his radio and whispers, "Beta team leader to alpha team leader. We're in the computer core and are about to start placing the charges."

"Roger that, beta team leader."

Beta team is alone in the computer core, so they quickly place the twenty explosive charges all over the equipment in the room. Every piece of equipment has a charge stuck to it. They like to be thorough.

Lieutenant Grayson activates his radio again and whispers, "Beta team leader to alpha team leader. We have finished placing the charges and are heading back to the landing bay."

"Roger that, beta team leader. Notify me when you're back in the landing bay."

"Roger that, alpha team leader."

It only takes a few minutes for Lieutenant Grayson's team to get back to the landing bay. Amazingly, they don't run in to a single Xandurian on the way.

As they enter the bay, Lieutenant Grayson activates his radio and whispers, "Beta team leader to alpha team leader. We're back in the landing bay."

"Roger that, beta team leader."

Beta team has only been back in the landing bay for a minute when the large landing bay doors start to open. They see a ship, very similar to the one they arrived in, approaching the bay.

Lieutenant Grayson activates his radio and whispers, "Beta team leader to alpha team leader. You're not going to believe this, but the real Xandurian guard shift change is here early. You need to hurry."

"Fuck! Roger that, beta team leader."

Alpha team has already placed the explosives around the lab, but they still need to place the explosives on the time machine itself. They need to make sure it is destroyed. Unfortunately, they no longer have the time to casually walk around the time machine to place the explosives. They now have to deviate from the original plan and switch to their backup plan. The original plan was to plant the charges, leave the lab and detonate the explosives before the Xandurians realized what was going on. Their backup plan is..., a little messier.

Lieutenant Stephens radios his team members and whispers, "Heads up, alpha team, we are switching to Plan B in five... four... three... two... one... execute."

The eight members of his team drop their holograms, target the scientists in the room with their pulse rifles and begin firing. It takes several shots to kill each Xandurian scientist and there are more than a dozen scientists in the lab, but the team takes them all out before any of them could set off the alarms. They reactivate their holograms and quickly place the rest of the explosive charges on the time machine. After that they all exit the lab and run for the elevator.

Lieutenant Stephens activates his radio and whispers, "Alpha team leader to beta team leader, we're on our way down to the landing bay."

"Roger that, alpha team leader. We have taken up a defensive position around the ship. I suggest you haul ass."

It's at that point that the alarms go off all over the Xandurian base. One of the scientific team's support technicians walked into the science lab, found all the scientists dead and set off the security alarms.

As the elevator doors open on the landing bay level, Lieutenant Stephens pulls out the remote detonator and pushes the button with his thumb. The base rocks and the massive explosions can be heard throughout the whole facility.

Back in the landing bay the ship carrying the real Xandurian guard shift change has just landed, and the loading ramp is lowering. The twenty Xandurian guards stream out of the ship just as alpha team enters the landing bay.

Lieutenant Stephens says, "Okay, everyone, run for the ship."

Looking at him, Lieutenant Stephens can tell that the Xandurian commanding officer is suspicious about what he sees in the landing bay. Ten soldiers in a defensive formation around a ship in the landing bay, and ten more soldiers running towards the ship. With the base under attack, the soldiers should run towards the fight not away from it. The Xandurian commander approaches and yells at Lieutenant Stephens while pointing towards the main corridor.

Lieutenant Stephens couldn't understand what the Xandurian was saying, but he knew they were in trouble, so without breaking his stride he raises his pulse rifle and shoots the Xandurian in the chest at point blank range as he passes. The blast sends the Xandurian flying, he lands on his back and slides across the floor. He is motionless when he comes to a stop.

Lieutenant Stephens yells, "OPEN FIRE!"

Both teams open fire on the rest of the Xandurian security squad. A few Xandurians go down immediately and the rest take cover behind the various crates and barrels in the landing bay and return fire.

Alpha team reaches their ship and joins beta team in their defensive formation. Some have taken cover behind the landing gear, some have taken cover behind the loading ramp, and some are laying on the deck in the prone position.

Up in the flight deck of the ship, Lieutenant Hamersley has been watching, so he opens fire with the ship's laser cannons and is able to pick off several Xandurians.

Just when he thinks they have taken out enough of the Xandurians so the teams can board the ship and they can take off, dozens upon dozens of Xandurian soldiers stream into the landing bay and join the fire fight. The odds are quickly tipping in the Xandurians' favor.

Due to the sheer volume of energy blasts coming from the now overwhelming Xandurian force in the landing bay, Lieutenant Stephens' and Lieutenant Grayson's men fall one by one. It is quickly becoming apparent that they won't escape from the Xandurian base. With only half a dozen men left in the fire fight Lieutenant Stephens realizes he needs to ensure that none of the men are captured and tortured. He knows it is time to engage the failsafe.

Before the captured Xandurian ship left Earth, it was loaded with half a dozen high yield, cold fusion bombs. Should something go wrong, the team could land one final blow and take a lot of Xandurians with them. Lieutenant Stephens pulls out the remote and arms the cold fusion bombs. Two more of his men get hit, leaving just himself and three others. He lets out a death yell as loud as he can and pushes the button with his thumb.

All the video feeds from inside the station suddenly cut off. However, the video feeds from the cloaked satellites continue to stream showing the aftermath of the detonation. The landing bay is pretty much at the center of the asteroid, so the massive explosion not only obliterates the base, it shatters the asteroid into half a dozen large pieces and millions of small pieces.

Several of the large pieces destroy four of the Xandurian war ships that were patrolling close to the asteroid. Some fast moving smaller pieces of the asteroid blast right through a few other Xandurian war ships that were a little farther away.

These fast moving asteroid chunks cause massive damage to these ships, disabling them and setting them adrift.

Admiral Daniels stands and says, “I would like a moment of silence to honor the twenty-one outstanding soldiers that lost their lives today and to thank them for their sacrifice.”

Everyone in the room stands and bows their heads to show their respect for the fallen men.

After a minute Admiral Daniels says, “Thank you, all.”

Everyone in the command center turns and files out without saying a word.

Chief Tanner, Nathan and his crew head over to the elevators, take one down to the ground floor and head back to their police cars.

They get in the cars and start the trip back to police headquarters. Nathan and Mr. Black slowly pull up to and then turn left onto the main street in front of EDF headquarters. They drive back to police headquarters, this time with no lights and sirens.

It’s a quiet drive back, everyone is in a solemn mood. Nobody feels like talking about what they just witnessed. Twenty-one brave soldiers laid down their lives in order to prevent an alien species from finishing what could have amounted to the ultimate weapon. A weapon that could have been used to travel back into the past to wipe out Earth and the human race, removing them from history.

Though they feel sadness for the men that lost their lives and for the families they left behind, there is also a feeling of relief. The Xandurian threat has been looming over everything like a shadow for several months now. For the first time in quite a while the sun is out, and the shadow is gone.

When they arrive back at police headquarters, they return the cars to the secure underground parking area.

The chief shakes Nathan's hand and says, "I'm going to go home and drink to those soldiers. I suggest you and your team do the same. Then we'll get back at it tomorrow."

"Excellent idea, Chief. Have a good evening."

The chief nods at Nathan and then heads back into police headquarters. Nathan and his crew walk over to their police cruiser sitting on the helipad.

As they approach the front of the ship Nathan says, "Vanessa unlock and open the lower ramp."

Vanessa's voice comes over the external speakers, "Aye Captain Stone, opening the lower ramp now."

Once open, everyone walks up the ramp into the ship and then they head up to the bridge. Everyone takes their seats and prep the ship for takeoff.

When the ship is ready Nathan says, "Ms. Arnoult, contact Seattle air traffic control and request clearance for takeoff."

"Aye Captain."

"Mr. Black, plot a course for Jasper."

"Aye Captain."

"Mr. Bell, fire up the engines."

"Aye Captain."

The crew hears the jet engines spin up and start.

Moments later Desiree says, "Captain, Seattle air traffic control has granted us clearance for a vertical takeoff, no traffic in the immediate area."

"Thank you, Ms. Arnoult."

"Mr. Bell, take us home."

"Aye Captain."

Mr. Bell pushes the throttles half way open, and the ship begins to rise. When the ship reaches two hundred feet, Mr.

Bell adjusts the thrust vectoring, and the ship starts to move forward. Mr. Bell rams the throttles wide open after which the ship accelerates and climbs rapidly, pushing the crew back in their seats. In just a few minutes the ship is up at thirty thousand feet and cruising at five hundred knots.

"Captain, we have reached cruising altitude and speed, we should arrive in Jasper in approximately one hour."

"Thank you, Mr. Bell."

Mr. Black turns around and asks Nathan, "So what do you think the Xandurians will do now, Captain?"

"I think we can expect a retaliatory strike at either Trynx 3 or Earth or both. We'll just have to wait and see."

An hour later as they are getting close to Jasper, Nathan says, "Ms. Arnoult, contact Jasper air traffic control, request an approach vector and get us clearance to land on my helipad."

"Aye Captain."

A few moments later Ms. Arnoult says, "Captain, Jasper air traffic control has sent us an approach vector and granted us clearance for a vertical landing on your helipad. I have sent the approach vector to Mr. Black's console."

"Thank you, Ms. Arnoult."

Mr. Black reviews the data and says, "Confirmed, approach vector laid in, Captain."

"Thank you, Mr. Black."

"Mr. Bell, take us down."

"Aye Captain."

As they approach Nathan's home in Jasper, Mr. Bell slows the ship down to a crawl and lines it up with the helipad.

Soon the ship is hovering at two hundred feet directly over the helipad beside Nathan's house. Mr. Bell pulls back on the throttles a little more and the ship descends slowly. When the ship has descended to fifty feet, the landing gear comes down. A few moments later the wheels touch the ground and Mr. Bell shuts the engines down.

Nathan stands up and says, "Nice smooth landing, Mr. Bell."

"Thank you, Captain."

"All right everyone, shut everything down and let's go."

The crew finishes shutting down the ship's systems and then they make their way down to the lower bay. They open the ramp, walk out onto the helipad and then head into the house. One by one they grab a beer from the refrigerator in the kitchen and then head out onto the deck.

Nathan is the last one out of the house and when he has joined the others, he holds his beer up and says, "To the twenty-one brave soldiers that gave their lives this day so we can be safe."

The rest of the crew raise their beers, clink the bottles together and all say, "Here here."

Nathan lights a fire in the fire pit on the deck as it gets cool this time of year in Jasper. They spend the next hour drinking beer on the deck before making dinner. After dinner they head inside, make a big batch of popcorn, grab themselves another drink and settle in the theater room to watch an old science fiction movie. Something they haven't done in months. After the movie, everyone heads off to bed. Nathan crawls into bed, snuggles up next to Desiree, and for the first time in a long time falls asleep quickly and sleeps soundly. Life is returning to normal.

# CHAPTER 7 – BETRAYAL AND REVENGE

Nathan wakes around one o'clock in the morning and he immediately senses that something is wrong. His heart rate rises sharply, he feels the heaviness that is fear in the pit of his stomach, adrenaline pumps through his body and he realizes that his skin is coated with a thin veil of sweat.

The moonlight streaming through the window gives his bedroom an almost eerie feeling. He sits up in bed and looks around the room. Just behind the beam of moonlight, in the shadows, he can make out the silhouette of a person sitting in a chair near the foot of his bed.

With his heart pounding in his chest he says, "Who's there?"

Whomever or whatever is sitting in the chair stands up and slowly steps around the bed moving closer to the window.

Another blast of adrenaline is released into Nathan's bloodstream.

The first thing Nathan sees is the barrel of a blaster as it breaks the beam of moonlight. With another step the whole blaster with an alien hand holding it emerges from the shadows. With one final step the right side of the alien's upper body and face becomes bathed in the moonlight. The rest of him remains in shadow.

Nathan can now make out who or rather what has invaded his bedroom. It's a Xandurian, a big one, he's at least seven feet six inches tall.

Nathan's eyes go from the Xandurian's face to the blaster pointing at him and back to his face. Trying to stay calm Nathan slowly reaches over to Desiree's side of the bed to wake her, but finds she is not in bed with him. Only his training and years of experience keeps him from panicking.

The Xandurian holds up a small device and begins to speak. Out of the device comes the English translation, "Can you understand me, Captain Stone?"

"Yes, I can understand you."

"Good."

"What do you want?"

"Oh, I think that should be obvious, Captain Stone. I want the ore from Trynx 3 and you're going to bring it to me."

"And just why would I do that?"

"Because, Captain Stone, we have your female. If you want her back alive and unharmed you will do exactly as I say. If you don't, I will send her back to you piece by piece. Do you understand me, Captain Stone?"

After hearing this, Nathan's subconscious tenses up all the muscles of his body and curl his hands into tight fists.

Gritting his teeth together he says, "Yes, I understand you."

"Good."

The Xandurian throws Nathan a small device and says, "You have seventy-two of your Earth hours to bring me a crate full of the ore. The rendezvous coordinates are on this device. Oh and come alone or the female dies."

The Xandurian turns to walk out when Nathan says, "One question before you go."

"Very well, what is your question?"

"What do you need the time ore for? We destroyed your time machine and the lab it was being developed in."

A slight, but evil grin appears on the Xandurian's face, but he says nothing.

"That wasn't the real lab was it? The time machine was a fake wasn't it?"

"Very good, Captain Stone. Did you really think we would just let you blow up our time machine? Oh, your plan was quite effective, I will give you that. What a shame that your brave men sacrificed their lives and accomplished nothing."

Nathan can feel the anger boiling up inside him. His muscles tense up even more. He looks at the Xandurian with utter hatred in his eyes and says, "I wouldn't say we accomplished nothing. We killed several thousand of your people and I promise you they won't be the last."

"We'll see, Captain Stone, we'll see."

The Xandurian turns and walks down the hallway yelling back over his shoulder, "Oh, and don't bother looking for your female here on Earth, she's not here."

Nathan jumps out of bed, grabs a blaster from his night stand drawer, runs down the hallway after the Xandurian and yells, "COME BACK HERE YOU FUCKING FISH FACED, BLUE, SON OF A BITCH!"

Awoken by the commotion in the hallway, Mr. Black, Mr. Bell, Ms. Norata and Mr. Nagata all come out of their bedrooms in various stages of dress brandishing their blasters.

By the time Nathan gets outside the Xandurian has already stepped on the boarding ramp of the small transport waiting for him. The transport immediately climbs and flies away even before the ramp has closed.

Nathan gets off a few shots with his blaster before the transport is too far away, but he wasn't able to inflict any real damage. The rest of his crew runs outside too late to get off a single shot at the transport.

Nathan drops to his knees, looks up at the stars and screams as loudly as he can. He then gets bombarded by questions from his crew.

Mr. Black asks, "What the hell just happened?"

Mr. Bell asks, "Who the hell was that?"

Ms. Norata looks around and asks, "Where's Desiree?"

Nathan stands up slowly and says, "I woke up with a Xandurian sitting in my room. Desiree is gone. They took her."

"Oh my God! Why would they take Desiree?"

"To blackmail me into bringing them some of the Trynx 3 ore."

Mr. Black says, "Trynx 3 ore? Why would they need the Trynx 3 ore? We just destroyed... son of a bitch!"

Nathan says, "We blew up a decoy. A fake. They still have a time machine."

Nathan turns, walks back into the house and says, "Somebody make a big pot of coffee, we have a long night ahead of us. Lots of calls to make, lots of people to wake up."

Nathan follows standard protocol in this situation. This protocol is a direct response to an alien incursion on Earth.

The first thing he does is call and wake up Police Chief Tanner who, after getting over the initial shock, notifies the EDF of the incursion and the Xandurian time machine. The news is not received well by anyone.

As a preliminary precaution the planetary police send a team out to Nathan's home to scan for and remove any unauthorized surveillance equipment that the alien may have planted. The team arrives a few hours later and begins their sweep. The first thing they do is shut down all known electronic equipment in Nathan's home and then they scan for powered electronic devices. To everyone's astonishment, the team finds fifty micro cameras and fifty microphones throughout Nathan's home. They find another ten cameras and microphones in both the hangar and the garage. They find two cameras and microphones in each of Nathan's cars and they find another thirty cameras and microphones in the new police cruiser. They even found cameras and microphones in the trees around the property watching the yard and the exterior of the buildings.

The amount of surveillance equipment found is astonishing. Nathan and the members of his team were being watched constantly, every single thing they did was being recorded. Not one square inch of Nathan's home and property escaped surveillance.

This level of surveillance raises serious concerns at both the planetary police and the EDF who in turn perform the same type of scans throughout their respective headquarters. A number of micro cameras and microphones are found in key areas of both headquarters buildings.

Finding surveillance equipment in all three locations raises questions as to who could have slipped in unnoticed and planted the devices. Were they dealing with one perpetrator or several? Hopefully the investigation can solve the mystery quickly.

Now that the investigation is underway, Nathan can focus his attention on coming up with a plan to get Desiree back from the Xandurians without giving them any of the time ore. Being a brilliant strategist, it doesn't take Nathan long at all to come up with a plan.

Nathan presents his plan to his crew and then says, "Let's head to Seattle so I can present my plan to Chief Tanner."

His crew all answer with, "Aye Captain."

Nathan and his team head out to the helipad beside his house. As they approach the front of the ship Nathan says, "Vanessa, unlock and open the lower ramp."

Vanessa's voice comes over the external speakers, "Aye Captain Stone, opening the lower ramp now."

Once open, everyone walks up the ramp into the ship and then they head up to the bridge. Everyone takes their seats and begin to prep the ship for takeoff.

When they are ready Nathan says, "Vanessa, contact Jasper air traffic control and request clearance for takeoff."

“Aye Captain.”

“Mr. Black, plot a course to police headquarters in Seattle.”

“Aye Captain, course plotted and laid in.”

“Mr. Bell, fire up the engines.”

“Aye Captain.”

The crew hears the jet engines spin up and start.

Vanessa comes on and says, “Captain Stone, I have contacted Jasper air traffic control and they have granted us clearance for a vertical takeoff, no traffic in the immediate area.”

“Thank you, Vanessa.”

“Mr. Bell, take us up.”

“Aye Captain.”

Mr. Bell pushes the throttles half way open, and the ship begins to rise. When the ship reaches two hundred feet, he adjusts the thrust vectoring, and the ship starts to move forward. Mr. Bell rams the throttles wide open after which the ship accelerates and climbs rapidly, pushing the crew back in their seats. In just a few minutes the ship is up at thirty thousand feet and cruising at five hundred knots.

“Captain, we have reached cruising altitude and speed, we should arrive in Seattle in approximately one hour.”

“Thank you, Mr. Bell.”

A little over an hour later, as their ship approaches Seattle, Nathan says, “Vanessa, contact Seattle air traffic control and request the approach vector and clearance for a vertical landing at the Planetary Police headquarters helipad.”

“Aye Captain.”

A few moments later Vanessa says, “Captain, Seattle air traffic control has cleared us for landing at headquarters and has sent me the approach vector. I have sent the approach vector to Mr. Black's console."

"Thank you, Vanessa."

Mr. Black reviews the data and says, "Confirmed, approach vector laid in, Captain."

"Thank you, Mr. Black."

"Mr. Bell, take us down."

"Aye Captain."

Mr. Bell pulls back on the throttles, the ship descends, they break through the clouds and the vast city that is Seattle comes into view. As they approach Planetary Police headquarters, Mr. Bell slows the ship down and banks to port, turning around one hundred and eighty degrees. He slows the ship down to a crawl and lines it up with the helipad. Soon the ship is hovering at two hundred feet directly over the helipad. Mr. Bell pulls back on the throttles a little more and the ship descends slowly. When the ship reaches fifty feet, the landing gear comes down. Moments later the wheels touch the ground and Mr. Bell shuts the engines down.

Nathan stands up and says, "Nice smooth landing, Mr. Bell."

"Thank you, Captain."

"You all stay here, I'll be back soon."

Nathan makes his way from the bridge down to the lower bay where he opens the ramp and walks out onto the helipad. He walks over to and enters police headquarters and then takes the elevator up to the top floor where Chief Tanner's office is located. He makes his way from the elevators to Chief Tanner's office.

As he walks into the chief's office, the chief comes out from behind his desk, shakes Nathan's hand and says, "Captain Stone, I'm so sorry about Ms. Arnoult."

"Thank you, Chief."

"Please sit down and let's hear your plan to get her back."

Nathan sits down and begins to layout his plan for the chief.

After hearing the plan Chief Tanner says, "Sounds like a simple enough plan, but we will have to run it past Fleet Admiral Daniels at the EDF."

The chief calls over to EDF headquarters and speaks with Admiral Daniels regarding a meeting to go over Nathan's plan. The admiral has some time open in his schedule, so he agrees to a meeting at Planetary Police headquarters in an hour.

When Admiral Daniels arrives, he is shown into the chief's office where Chief Tanner and Nathan are waiting for him. They stand to greet the admiral as he comes in.

Chief Tanner shakes Admiral Daniels' hand and says, "Thank you for coming, Admiral."

"Of course, Chief Tanner."

Nathan says, "Thank you for coming on such short notice, Admiral, this operation is time sensitive."

"Captain Stone, one of your crew's lives is at risk, I'll do whatever I can to help with her recovery. So, what have you come up with?"

Nathan lays out his plan for the admiral after which the Admiral says, "Sounds pretty simple to me, Captain Stone, you have my approval. I'll set the wheels in motion on my side of things. I'll call Colonel Williamson on Trynx 3 and get your ore on a transport. You should have it in about six hours."

All three men stand up and Nathan shakes the admiral's hand, "Thank you, Admiral."

"Good luck and God speed, Captain."

Chief Tanner shakes the admiral's hand, "Thank you, Admiral."

"Chief Tanner, always a pleasure."

The admiral turns and walks out of the chief's office and heads back to EDF headquarters.

Nathan turns and shakes the chief's hand and says, "Thank you, Chief."

"Good luck, Captain Stone."

Nathan turns and leaves the chief's office, heads over to the elevators and takes one down to the ground floor. He exits the building and walks over to the helipad where his crew is waiting for him in their police cruiser. Nathan walks up the open ramp and continues on up to the bridge.

Upon entering the bridge Nathan says, "Okay, Chief Tanner and Admiral Daniels approved my plan. We've got about six hours before the ore we need arrives from Trynx 3 so let's use that time to check and recheck every system on this ship. This will be our first time going into battle with her so let's make sure she's ready."

Everyone answers, "Aye Captain."

The crew spends the next six hours going through the ship from stem to stern while Nathan prepares to execute his plan.

When the transport carrying the crate of ore arrives from Trynx 3, it lands at EDF headquarters. The crate is then loaded in the back of an armored assault vehicle. It, along with several other heavily armed escort vehicles, begins a fifteen minute drive over to the Planetary Police headquarters. The trip goes without incident and the convoy is soon pulling up to Nathan's police cruiser sitting on the helipad.

Nathan is working in the lower bay of the police cruiser so one of the helipad ground crew yells up the ramp that a convoy of heavily armed military vehicles has just pulled up. Nathan drops what he's doing and walks down the ramp to take possession of the crate of ore.

A young lieutenant pulls the crate out of the back of the armored assault vehicle and then he, accompanied by a dozen soldiers armed with heavy pulse rifles, brings the crate to the edge of the helipad where Nathan is waiting.

The young lieutenant says, "Captain Stone, I was instructed to deliver this crate to you, sir."

"Thank you, Lieutenant. Before you hand me the crate would you like to see my identification?"

"No need, Captain Stone, every officer that graduates from the academy has had to study your record and your tactics extensively. I know who you are, and I recognize you from the photos of you in your service record, sir. May I also say it is an honor to meet you, sir?"

"Ah, yes, of course, Lieutenant. Thank you."

"Here is your crate, Captain Stone."

Nathan takes the crate of ore from the young lieutenant and says, "Thank you, Lieutenant."

"My pleasure, sir."

The lieutenant and his men return to their vehicles and drive off, heading back to EDF headquarters.

Nathan takes the crate of ore up the ramp and into the lower bay of his police cruiser. He closes the ramp behind him and then heads up to the bridge to join the rest of his crew.

After taking his seat Nathan says, "Vanessa, contact Seattle air traffic control and request clearance for takeoff and then contact Earth space flight control and get us clearance for space flight."

"Aye Captain."

"Mr. Bell, fire up the engines."

"Aye Captain."

The crew hears the jet engines spin up and start.

Moments later Vanessa says, "Captain, Seattle air traffic control has granted us clearance for a vertical takeoff and

Earth space flight control has granted us clearance for space flight. Both report no traffic in the immediate area."

"Thank you, Vanessa."

"Mr. Bell, take us up."

"Aye Captain."

Mr. Bell pushes the throttles half way open, and the ship begins to rise. When the ship reaches two hundred feet, he adjusts the thrust vectoring, and the ship starts to move forward. Mr. Bell rams the throttles wide open after which the ship accelerates and climbs rapidly, pushing the crew back in their seats. Several minutes after takeoff, the sky around the ship turns black as they near the edge of the planet's atmosphere. At this point Mr. Bell disengages the jet engines and closes the air intakes. He then engages the sub-light engines and rams the throttles wide open. The ship accelerates, almost violently, to achieve escape velocity.

Vanessa announces, "Now leaving Earth's gravity. Artificial gravity plating is coming online."

"Mr. Black, plot a course for the rendezvous coordinates."

"Aye Captain, course laid in."

"Mr. Bell, take us to the rendezvous coordinates, 14 TSL."

"Aye Captain."

The ship accelerates rapidly away from Earth, and soon the crew sees the bright blue flash of light through the bridge windows as the ship enters FTL.

After a few minutes Mr. Bell says, "Captain, we have reached 14 TSL. Estimated time to the rendezvous coordinates is approximately forty-eight hours."

"Thank you, Mr. Bell."

Nathan thinks to himself, "At 14 TSL it will take them approximately forty-eight hours to reach the rendezvous coordinates. We're cutting it very close."

The next two days are especially long for Nathan. He is anxious and nervous and all he can think about is getting there as fast as he can and getting Desiree back. He also has trouble sleeping and doesn't have much of an appetite.

After what seems like an eternity of watching stars streak past through the bridge windows, they are finally getting close to the rendezvous coordinates.

A series of beeps comes from his console and then Mr. Black says, "Captain, one minute to the rendezvous coordinates."

Nathan says, "Thank you, Mr. Black."

"Ms. Norata, anything on the sensors?"

"No, Captain, nothing on sensors. No ships in the area."

"Thank you, Ms. Norata."

"Mr. Bell, drop us out of FTL."

"Aye Captain, dropping us out of FTL now."

The crew sees a bright blue flash of light through the bridge windows as the police cruiser drops out of FTL.

Nathan says, "Mr. Bell, all stop."

"Aye Captain, all stop."

After dropping out of FTL and seeing that there is no one waiting for them, just a lot of empty space, Nathan checks the time and sees they have arrived a little early, so they have no choice but to sit and wait for the Xandurians to arrive.

After about half an hour Ms. Norata's console lights up red and an alarm goes off, "Captain, there are twenty-five ships approaching our position in FTL, ten seconds out."

"Very well, Ms. Norata, shields up at full power in reflective mode, and bring the weapons systems online."

"Aye Captain, shields up at full power in reflective mode, and the weapons are online."

The twenty-five Xandurian ships drop out of FTL in a large arrowhead pattern with the lead ship coming to a full stop directly in front of Nathan's cruiser about one kilometer away.

A minute later Vanessa says, "Captain, we have an incoming transmission from the Xandurians."

Nathan stands up, takes a few steps forward and says, "On screen, Vanessa."

The front view screen activates and displays the lead Xandurian ship's bridge with the captain front and center. Nathan believes this is the same Xandurian that was in his house three days ago.

The Xandurian says in a smug tone with a grin on his face "Nice to see you again, Captain Stone, I'm so glad you made it on time."

Nathan doesn't react at all other than to say, "Let's get on with it, shall we?"

"Very well, quick and to the point. I like that about you, Captain Stone. Here's how this is going to work. We will send over a small drone. You will place the crate of ore on the drone and then the drone will return to my ship. Once we have the ore and verify its authenticity, we will send your female back to you in a shuttle."

Nathan says, "Very well, but I want to see Desiree first."

"Very well, Captain Stone."

The Xandurian captain turns and nods to one of his subordinates who then leaves the bridge. He returns a minute later with Desiree in tow, her hands bound in front of her with some sort of hand cuffs. He guides her over to stand beside the captain.

"Well as you can see, Captain Stone, she is alive and well."

"Are you okay, Desiree? Have they harmed you in any way?"

"Yes, I'm okay Nathan, they haven't harmed me."

"Don't worry, sweetheart, we'll have you back in no time."

Nathan looks back at the Xandurian Captain and says, "Send over your drone. I will open the landing bay doors and deliver the crate of ore myself." Nathan pushes a button on his command console cutting off the transmission.

Nathan exits the bridge, heads to the shuttle bay at the stern of the ship and opens the bay doors.

A few minutes later the Xandurian drone flies through the atmospheric force field and into the shuttle bay. The drone sets down in the center of the bay and waits for Nathan to load the crate of ore. The rear section of the drone consists of a small flat deck with four mechanical arms, one on each corner. Nathan puts the crate of ore on the drone's deck and the four mechanical arms clamp down on it to hold it in place. Immediately after that, the drone lifts off, it turns one hundred and eighty degrees and blasts out of the landing bay at high speed.

Nathan closes the bay doors and then makes his way back up to the bridge.

Nathan and his crew watch the drone fly back to the lead Xandurian ship and into one of its landing bays.

Nathan says, "Vanessa, hail the lead Xandurian ship."

"Aye Captain."

A few moments later she says, "Captain, I have the Xandurian commander for you again."

"On screen, Vanessa."

"Aye Captain."

The main view screen activates and the Xandurian commander appears once again.

Nathan says, "Okay, Xandurian, you have the ore, now it's your turn. Return my crew member immediately."

"Not so fast, Captain Stone. The crate of ore you sent over is being brought up to the bridge as we speak. It must be verified before I return your female."

"Very well, Xandurian."

A few minutes later Nathan and his crew see the crate being carried onto the Xandurian bridge. The Xandurian captain takes it from lower ranked officer and sets it on his command console.

Another Xandurian comes over with a pry bar looking tool and some type of hand held scanning device. He pries the top off the crate with the pry bar and then picks up the scanning device. He scans the crate for a few seconds, reads the results on the scanner's display and then nods his head at the commander.

The commander looks up at Nathan and says, "You kept your word, Captain Stone. You surprise me. I expected some type of deception."

"You got what you wanted, Xandurian, now return my crew member."

"I'm afraid that's not possible, Captain Stone."

"What do you mean that's not possible?"

"What I mean is she's not your crew member. She's not even a real person. She is a cybernetic organism we created. She was planted in your organization several years ago to provide intelligence to facilitate the acquisition of the Trynx 3 ore to power our time machine."

Nathan and his crew are in shock over what they have just heard. Nathan stands there silent while the other four call the Xandurian a liar in several ways in angry tones.

Nathan yells over them, "QUIET, ALL OF YOU!"

He looks back at the Xandurian and says, "I don't believe it."

"Oh, it is quite true, Captain Stone, and I can prove it."

The Xandurian nods at Desiree who releases herself from the hand cuffs, grabs her left wrist with her right hand, gives it a quick sharp twist, pulls it away from her left forearm and exposes the internal electronics.

Ms. Norata gasps in shock and covers her nose and mouth with her hands. A few tears roll down her cheeks.

Both Mr. Bell and Mr. Black say, "Oh my God," at the same time.

Nathan plops down in his chair and holds his head in his hands, his elbows on his knees. He can't believe what he has just seen and is trying to process the depth of this deception.

"Didn't you ever wonder why 'Desiree' so wanted to meet you and to be placed on your team? We programmed her to make that happen any way she could. It was a lot easier than we thought."

Nathan looks up, dragging his hands down his face in disbelief, anger welling up inside him and says, "Well at least now we know how the cameras and microphones got planted in my house, Planetary Police headquarters and the EDF headquarters."

"Yes, Captain Stone, we've been one step ahead of you the whole time thanks to 'Desiree' here."

"How can that be? If that were true then how did we surprise the Sulari, wipe them out and save Earth?"

"Ah yes, the Sulari. That's simple, Captain Stone, we let you wipe them out. We found out through similar surveillance techniques that the Sulari were planning on stealing our time machine and taking the Trynx 3 ore for themselves to carry out their own agenda. We couldn't allow that to happen."

"I have to say, Captain Stone you surprise me. Considering your reputation, you were more gullible than we could have possibly imagined. All it took was a nice pair of breasts and a sexually aggressive personality to give us the upper hand."

The Xandurian captain picks up the crate of ore and says, "And now we have the ore we need to power our time machine. Thanks to you, Captain Stone."

With the anger boiling up in him Nathan spits, "That may be, but as the Sulari found out I am a brilliant tactician and I never go into any situation without a tactical advantage."

"You have no tactical advantage here and now, you are a fool, Captain Stone."

Nathan's anger boils over. He stands up, and with his right hand picks up the remote detonator from his command console and shows it to the Xandurian, "You may think that, asshole, but I'm not the one holding a crate packed with extremely high yield explosives."

The Xandurian looks down at the crate in his hands and then looks back at Nathan with a panicked look on his face.

Nathan looks at Desiree, she may be a machine, but she looks terrified.

"Goodbye, Desiree."

Nathan pushes the button on the top of the detonator with his thumb.

The Xandurian yells, "Nooooooooo," but is cut off when the crate he is holding explodes.

The massive explosion tears the whole front of the Xandurian ship off. The initial explosion sets off a series of cascading explosions. The cascading explosions hit the main reactor which culminates in a massive explosion that vaporizes the entire ship.

The other twenty-four Xandurian ships open fire on Nathan's cruiser. Hundreds of laser cannon blasts are bouncing off the police cruiser's shields.

With the ship shaking from the weapons impacts Nathan sits down and yells, "Ms. Norata, target the closest ships and fire at will. Give them everything you've got."

“Aye Captain, targets acquired, firing.”

Ms. Norata fires several salvos of missiles, the Gatling lasers, the laser turrets and the particle beam weapons at the two closest Xandurian ships. Nathan’s crew watches as their weapons impact the shields of the two Xandurian ships, but don’t cause any visible damage.

The little police cruiser is getting pummeled by the twenty-four Xandurian ships. The ship is shaking violently which is causing damage to the ship’s systems and to its structure. Sparks are flying from computer panels, power conduits and several of the stations around the bridge. The crew is holding onto their chairs and consoles to avoid being tossed about.

Ms. Norata says, “Captain, our shields can only take so much of this.”

Nathan pushes a button on the command console on his chair to activate the comm system and says, “Now, Admiral.”

Directly astern of Nathan’s cruiser, six dreadnoughts, four battle carriers, fifty heavy cruisers and fifty light cruisers decloak.

Nathan’s police cruiser stops shaking soon after as the Xandurian captains all retrain their weapons on the EDF fleet and open fire.

Nathan says, “Mr. Bell, evasive maneuvers. Get us out of the line of fire.”

“Aye Captain, evasive maneuvers.”

Mr. Bell banks the ship to starboard and drops the ship down beneath both fleets. Now that they are safely out of the way, the EDF ships open fire with their massive laser cannons.

Nathan hits a button on the command console on his chair and changes the main view screen so they can see the Xandurian fleet. They watch the massive red bolts of energy released by the EDF’s laser cannons impact the shields of the Xandurian ships.

It's not going to take long before the Xandurian's shields are drained and their ships incur major damage. With the odds being more than two to one for the EDF, this battle won't last long. The Xandurian captains have made a serious error in judgment trying to stand toe to toe with the big guns of the EDF fleet.

Mr. Bell has brought the ship around one hundred and eighty degrees and is heading back underneath the EDF fleet.

Ms. Norata's tactical console lights up red and an alarm sounds. She looks down to see there is a ship approaching their position in FTL.

"Captain, there's a single ship approaching our position in FTL."

Nathan pushes a button on the command console on his chair and changes the main view screen to display the bow camera once again.

A few moments later, a lone Xandurian ship drops out of FTL about one hundred meters away directly in front of them. The Xandurian ship is facing away from them so they cannot see Nathan's ship approaching from behind.

Nathan sees the ship has two damaged engines and some major hull damage. He immediately recognizes it as the ship with the bladed plasma energy weapon.

Nathan yells, "MS. NORATA, TARGET THAT SHIP AND FIRE EVERYTHING YOU'VE GOT AT THAT SON OF A BITCH! LIGHT HIM UP!"

"Aye Captain, missiles locked.... firing."

Ms. Norata quickly fires two missile salvos and then sets to work targeting the Gatling lasers, the laser turrets and the particle beam weapons at the Xandurian ship.

The first salvo of missiles destroys the remaining two starboard side thrusters on the rear of the ship. The second salvo of missiles hits dead center on the stern of the ship and blows the long trailing tail and starboard side vertical thruster strut clean off the ship. The ship starts to spin on its Z axis like it is out of control.

Nathan stands up from his chair and yells, "THEY FLEW INTO BATTLE WITH NO SHIELDS! FIRE AT WILL! TAKE THEM OUT!"

Ms. Norata says, "Aye Captain," and then launches salvo after salvo of missiles. She fires the Gatling lasers, followed by the laser turrets, followed by the particle beam weapons.

Nathan and his crew watch as their weapons impact the hull of the Xandurian ship. The missiles and laser turrets are blowing large pieces off the hull, the particle beam weapons are slicing through the hull like a hot knife through butter and the Gatling lasers are chewing away thousands of smaller pieces of the hull.

Nathan says, "Mr. Bell, side slip us in a large circle around the Xandurian ship while keeping our nose and the weapons bearing on the target."

"Aye Captain."

"Ms. Norata, continue firing."

"Aye Captain."

The police cruiser begins its first pass around the Xandurian ship. The Xandurian ship is taking quite a pounding and has not fired a single retaliatory shot, its weapons must be disabled.

Nathan is especially enjoying watching the Gatling lasers with their high cyclic rate chewing the hull to pieces.

As the police cruiser begins its second pass Nathan says, "Ms. Norata, as we come around the bow of that ship, I want you to fire four full spreads of missiles directly into their bridge."

"Aye Captain."

As they side slip past the bow of the Xandurian ship Ms. Norata fires the four missile salvos. Each salvo comprises four missiles so there are now sixteen missiles in total heading towards the enemy bridge. With only two seconds between each missile salvo the Xandurian ship is rocked by one massive explosion after another. These explosions have set off a series of cascading explosions inside the Xandurian ship.

Nathan says, "Mr. Bell, put some distance between us and them."

"Aye Captain."

Mr. Bell pulls the ship out of its side slip and banks to port, veering away from the Xandurian ship.

Nathan pushes a button on the command console on his chair and changes the main view screen to display the stern camera. They can see multiple explosions going off inside the Xandurian ship followed by a massive explosion that completely vaporizes the ship. Everyone on the bridge claps and cheers.

Nathan brings his right arm up in front of him, clenches his fist and pumps his arm in victory, "YES!"

When the explosion clears Nathan falls into his chair and says, "That's for Carter, you son of a bitch."

"Mr. Bell, bring us about so we can see how the fleet is doing."

"Aye Captain."

Nathan pushes a button on the command console on his chair and changes the main view screen to display the bow camera once again, and Mr. Bell turns the ship in the fleet's direction. They turn just in time to see four more Xandurian ships explode. There are only five Xandurian ships left and they are heavily damaged. The EDF fleet continues to fire their massive laser cannons, but the remaining Xandurian ships have already turned to retreat. They accelerate away rapidly and disappear in bright blue flashes of light as they jump into FTL.

Just then Vanessa says, “Captain Stone, we have an incoming transmission from the fleet.”

“On screen, Vanessa.”

Admiral Anderson on the Aurora appears on the screen, “Well we taught them a lesson or two didn’t we, Captain Stone?”

“Yes, Admiral, we certainly did. While you were busy with their fleet, we took out the prototype ship with the bladed plasma energy weapon. No more surprise attacks.”

“Excellent, Captain Stone. Payback is a wonderful thing.”

“It sure is, Admiral, it sure is.”

“Well that’s enough fun for one day, let’s head home.”

“Sounds good, Admiral. Stone out.”

Admiral Anderson disappears as the view screen changes from the bridge of the Aurora to displaying the fleet once again. The fleet breaks up, comes about one hundred and eighty degrees and accelerates away, disappearing in bright blue flashes of light.

Nathan says, “Mr. Black, plot a course for home.”

“Aye Captain, course laid in.”

“Mr. Bell, bring us about one hundred and eighty degrees, 14 TSL for home.”

“Aye Captain.”

Mr. Bell turns the ship around in a fairly tight arc and as soon as it hits the one hundred and eighty degree mark it accelerates away rapidly and jumps into FTL. The crew sees a bright blue flash of light through the bridge windows as the ship accelerates past the speed of light.

After a few minutes Mr. Bell says, “Captain, we have reached 14 TSL. Estimated time to the Earth is forty-eight hours.”

“Thank you, Mr. Bell.”

The trip back to Earth is a pretty solemn journey. The crew is still in shock over Desiree's deception. Nobody feels more betrayed than Nathan, but worse than that he is embarrassed that the Xandurians were able to deceive and manipulate him for well over a year, and who knows what secrets Desiree was able to acquire and send to the Xandurians.

Nathan is not mourning the loss of someone that he loved, he is angry. Angry at the Xandurians and angry at Desiree. Strangely enough Nathan takes solace knowing he was the instrument of her destruction.

Forty-eight hours later the EDF fleet arrives back at Earth, drops out of FTL and begins their approach to enter orbit of the planet.

On Nathan's police cruiser, a series of beeps comes from Mr. Black's console.

Mr. Black says, "Captain, one minute until we arrive at Earth."

Nathan says, "Thank you, Mr. Black."

"Mr. Bell, drop us out of FTL."

"Aye Captain, dropping us out of FTL now."

The crew sees a bright blue flash of light through the bridge windows as the police cruiser drops out of FTL.

The Earth instantly appears in the bridge windows and Nathan says, "Vanessa, contact Earth space flight control and get us clearance for re-entry and then contact Jasper air traffic control, request an approach vector and get us clearance to land on my helipad."

A few minutes later Vanessa says, "Captain, Earth space flight control has granted us clearance for re-entry. Jasper air traffic control has sent us an approach vector and granted us clearance for a vertical landing on your helipad. I have sent the approach vector to Mr. Black's console."

"Thank you, Vanessa."

Mr. Black reviews the data and says, "Confirmed, approach vector laid in, Captain."

"Thank you, Mr. Black."

"Mr. Bell, take us down."

"Aye Captain."

Mr. Bell noses the ship over and begins his descent into the atmosphere. The ship is descending over the Pacific Ocean, heading for the Canadian Rocky Mountains. As they approach Nathan's home in Jasper, Mr. Bell slows the ship down to a crawl and lines it up with the helipad. Soon the ship is hovering at two hundred feet directly over the helipad. Mr. Bell pulls back on the throttles and the ship descends slowly. When the ship has dropped to fifty feet, the landing gear comes down. A few moments later the wheels touch the ground and Mr. Bell shuts the engines down.

Nathan stands up and says, "Nice smooth landing, Mr. Bell."

"Thank you, Captain."

The crew finishes shutting down the ship's systems, then heads down to the lower bay, opens the ramp and walks out onto the helipad.

Nathan is the last one out and as he steps off the ramp says, "Vanessa, close and lock the ramp. Restricted access protocol."

Vanessa's voice comes over the external speakers, "Aye Captain, closing the ramp now. Restricted access protocol enabled."

The five of them head into the house. One by one they grab a beer from the refrigerator and then take a seat on the deck.

Nathan holds his beer up and says, "To payback."

The rest of the crew raise their beers and repeat, "To payback."

They all spend the next hour drinking beer on the deck. They talk about how gratifying it was destroying the ship with the bladed energy weapon.

Nathan and Ms. Norata hardly say a word, and nobody brings up the elephant in the room. Clearly Desiree's deception and death has affected Nathan and Ms. Norata the most.

After a couple of beers Nathan decides he needs something a little stronger, so he goes inside to the bar, grabs a short rocks glass and pours himself a scotch. Not just an ounce or two, a whole glass of scotch. He takes two steps back towards the deck then turns around and grabs the bottle to take it with him. He comes back outside and takes his seat again. The scotch in his glass doesn't last long.

The sun is going down behind the mountains and at this time of year it gets cool quickly so Nathan decides he should probably start a fire. In just a few minutes he has a nice warm fire burning and everyone has pulled their deck chairs a little closer.

A few minutes later Nathan realizes his back is still cold, so he goes inside and heads to his bedroom to grab a sweater. When he enters his room, he sees some of Desiree's belongings on the floor, on the bed, on her dresser and on the chaise lounge. A wave of emotion comes over him that is half anger and half sadness. Nathan goes with the anger. He runs downstairs, grabs a couple of boxes and then goes back to his room. He goes through everything in the bedroom, the closet and the en suite bathroom, and throws every item that belonged to Desiree into the boxes. He throws on the sweater he originally came to the bedroom to get, picks up the boxes and heads back out onto the deck.

His crew sees him come out with the boxes and watch as he walks past them to the stairs.

Nathan takes the stairs down to the ground, walks over to the large barrel he uses to burn garbage, and drops the boxes in. Without missing a step or looking back at his crew, Nathan walks over to the hangar, and goes inside. He heads over to the small arms locker at the rear of the hangar. He opens it and grabs two incendiary grenades. Nathan walks out of the hangar and heads back towards the burning barrel. As he approaches, he pulls the pins on the grenades. Without pause, Nathan casually drops the grenades in the barrel on top of Desiree's things as he walks past.

The grenades have a three second delay on them, so Nathan took about four steps before the grenades explode and start to burn.

Nathan continues with absolutely no reaction, up the stairs and back over to his deck chair. He sits down, pours himself another full glass of scotch, like nothing just happened, and says, "So what are we talking about?"

The next couple of days are pretty somber as the crew restocks, rearms and makes minor repairs to the police cruiser.

They don't see too much of Nathan. He is spending a lot of time driving his 1970 plum crazy purple Hemi Cuda convertible through the mountains with the top down, getting some sun, taking in the breath-taking view and trying to forget what happened a few short days ago.

# CHAPTER 8 – STARTING OVER

On the Monday after they arrived back in Jasper, Nathan is awakened at 06:00 hours by an incoming communication. He rolls over and touches the top of his nightstand to activate the screen on the wall in his bedroom.

Police Chief Tanner appears on the screen and says, "Sorry to wake you, Captain Stone, but I was just informed that a meeting has been called between the EDF and the Planetary Police to discuss the alien incursion and the continuing Xandurian threat. The meeting is at 08:00 hours this morning at the EDF headquarters here in Seattle. You better get moving if you don't want to be late."

Nathan yawns and rubs the sleep out of his eyes before saying, "Of course, Chief. I'll meet you in your office at 07:30 hours."

"Very well, Captain Stone, see you then. Tanner out."

The screen goes black and Nathan falls back on the bed and groans. He lays there in the dark for a few minutes not wanting to get up.

Finally, the little voice in his head says, "Come on, get up already."

Nathan rolls out of bed, throws on his robe, opens the bedroom door and heads down the hallway.

He knocks on Mr. Bell's door first and says, "Wake up, Mr. Bell, we have a meeting in Seattle at EDF headquarters at 08:00 hours. Let's go, mister."

Mr. Bell wakes and grumpily mumbles, "Okay, okay, I'm up, I'm up."

Nathan then wakes Mr. Black and Mr. Nagata, getting much the same grumpy response that Mr. Bell gave him.

Lastly Nathan knocks on Ms. Norata's door, "Wake up, Ms. Norata, we have a meeting in Seattle at EDF headquarters at 08:00 hours."

He gets no response from her, so he knocks a second time and says, "Ms. Norata?"

There is still no response so Nathan opens the door, knocks on it again and says, "Ms. Norata?"

Still no response so he pokes his head inside the room. The light from the hallway provides just enough light for Nathan to see that Ms. Norata had fallen asleep with a set of headphones on, probably listening to music. He also notices she is sleeping on her back with no covers on and that she is completely naked.

Shocked from seeing her naked, he freezes for a few seconds not knowing what to do. At the same time his eyes explore her naked body and he definitely likes what he sees. Ms. Norata is a beautiful, sexy, athletic woman and seeing her naked has made his mouth go dry.

After a few seconds he comes to his senses, steps into her room, tip toes over to her bed, grabs the sheet bunched up at her feet and begins to pull it up and over her. When the sheet is half way up her body, Nathan looks up to see that Ms. Norata's eyes are now open. Nathan freezes for a few seconds, not knowing what to do.

The little voice in Nathan's head finally says, "Finish pulling the sheet over her stupid."

He finishes pulling the sheet up and steps back. He is surprised at the way Ms. Norata has reacted. She wasn't scared when she woke up with a man standing over her, nor did she seem upset or embarrassed that Nathan had seen her totally naked. As a matter of fact, she seemed to have a seductive little grin on her face.

She simply pulls her headphones off, raises her upper body, leans back on her elbows and asks, "What can I do for you,

Captain?" while holding the same little seductive grin on her face.

Nathan nervously clears his throat and manages to squeak out, "Meeting... 08:00... EDF headquarters... Seattle... better get moving."

Neither of them says another word, Nathan backs out of her room and closes her door. In a daze he walks back to his room, closes the door and leans back against it. He stays there for a few seconds reflecting on what just happened then he straightens up and walks towards his bathroom. He looks down and sees he is fully erect and that his erection is sticking out of his robe.

In his head, the little voice says, "What the? Aww son of a bitch! I hope she didn't see that. You dope, you know she saw it. Why do you think she had that seductive little grin on her face? Son of a bitch!"

All five members of the crew get up, have a quick shower, get dressed and then meet in the kitchen for breakfast. Nathan is the last to enter the kitchen. The others are already sitting at the table having their coffee and eating their breakfast.

Nathan does his best to hide his embarrassment and avoid eye contact with Ms. Norata, but when he turns around after grabbing a coffee and a plate of food, his eyes lock with hers. She is sitting at the table with her arms crossed leaning on her elbows. She has that same seductive grin on her face and the look in her eyes is one of pure lust.

Suddenly Nathan feels very uncomfortable. He breaks their gaze and sits down at the other end of the table. He keeps his eyes down to avoid Ms. Norata's eyes, but he can feel her staring at him.

When everyone has finished breakfast, they quickly clean up the kitchen and then head out to the cruiser on the helipad.

It's now 07:00 hours in Jasper and 06:00 hours in Seattle. Nathan has an hour and a half until he is supposed to meet

Police Chief Tanner in his office at Planetary Police headquarters.

As they approach the front of the ship Nathan says, "Vanessa unlock and open the lower ramp."

Vanessa's voice comes over the external speakers, "Aye Captain Stone, opening the lower ramp now."

Once open, everyone walks up the ramp into the ship and then they head up to the bridge. Everyone takes their seats and begin to prep the ship for takeoff.

When they are ready Nathan says, "Vanessa, contact Jasper air traffic control and request clearance for takeoff."

"Aye Captain."

"Mr. Black, plot a course to police headquarters in Seattle."

"Aye Captain, course plotted and laid in."

"Mr. Bell, fire up the engines."

"Aye Captain."

The crew hears the jet engines spin up and start.

Vanessa comes on and says, "Captain, I have contacted Jasper air traffic control and they have granted us clearance for a vertical takeoff, no traffic in the immediate area."

Nathan responds with, "Thank you, Vanessa."

"Mr. Bell, take us up."

"Aye Captain."

Mr. Bell pushes the throttles half way open, and the ship begins to rise. When the ship reaches two hundred feet, he adjusts the thrust vectoring, and the ship starts to move forward. Mr. Bell rams the throttles wide open after which the ship accelerates and climbs rapidly, pushing the crew back in their seats. In just a few minutes the ship is up at thirty thousand feet and cruising at five hundred knots.

"Captain, we have reached cruising altitude and speed, we should arrive in Seattle in approximately one hour."

"Thank you, Mr. Bell."

It is a relatively quiet flight, as everyone is tired from going to bed late and being woken up so early. Some mornings not even strong coffee can fully wake you up.

Nathan gets comfortable in his chair, leaning on his left elbow, his chin resting in the palm of his hand. He has trouble keeping his eyes open and dozes off. He begins dreaming, replaying what took place in Ms. Norata's room earlier this morning only this time when he turns to leave Ms. Norata's room Desiree is standing there.

She looks down at Nathan's exposed erection then back up into his eyes and says, "You cheating bastard. You want her, don't you? Well you can't have her."

Desiree then cocks her right arm back like she's going to strike Nathan, but her arm has changed to a bright silver, metallic, mechanical arm with wires, hoses and hydraulic cylinders. She punches Nathan underneath his rib cage with an upper cut motion. He looks down to see that her arm has penetrated his flesh and is buried up to her elbow. She then rips her arm out of him, pulling his heart out and showing it to him.

This jolts Nathan awake, his heart pounding, and breathing heavy like he has just run a marathon. No more sleep for Nathan on this flight, he's wide awake now.

A little over an hour after lifting off from Jasper, as their ship approaches Seattle, Nathan says, "Vanessa, contact Seattle air traffic control and request the approach vector and clearance for a vertical landing at the Planetary Police headquarters helipad."

"Aye Captain."

A few moments later Vanessa says, "Captain, Seattle air traffic control has cleared us for landing at headquarters and has sent me the approach vector. I have sent the approach vector to Mr. Black's console."

"Thank you, Vanessa."

Mr. Black reviews the data and says, "Confirmed, approach vector laid in Captain."

"Thank you, Mr. Black."

"Mr. Bell, take us down."

"Aye Captain."

Mr. Bell pulls back on the throttles, the ship descends, they break through the clouds and the vast city that is Seattle comes into view. As they approach Planetary Police headquarters, Mr. Bell slows the ship down and banks to port, turning around one hundred and eighty degrees. He slows the ship down to a crawl and lines it up with the helipad. Soon the ship is hovering at two hundred feet directly over the helipad. Mr. Bell pulls back on the throttles a little more and the ship descends slowly. When the ship reaches fifty feet, the landing gear comes down. Moments later the wheels touch the ground and Mr. Bell shuts the engines down.

Nathan says, "Nice smooth landing Mr. Bell."

"Thank you, Captain."

The crew finishes shutting down the ship's systems, then heads down to the lower bay, opens the ramp and walks out onto the helipad.

Nathan is the last one out and as he steps off the ramp says, "Vanessa, close and lock the ramp. Restricted access protocol."

Vanessa's voice comes over the external speakers, "Aye Captain, closing the ramp now. Restricted access protocol enabled."

Mr. Bell, Mr. Black, Mr. Nagata and Ms. Norata are about five steps ahead of Nathan as they walk towards police headquarters. Nathan finds that his eyes keep wandering down to Ms. Norata's amazing backside, and he finds himself wondering what she's wearing under her skin tight flight uniform. When he finally tears his eyes away from her incredible backside, Nathan looks up to see that Ms. Norata is looking back over her shoulder at him. He knows he's been caught checking her out.

He can feel the heat in his face as it turns bright red and the little voice in his head says, "Good job, dumbass. Son of a bitch!"

Ms. Norata had caught Nathan checking out her butt. She giggles to herself seeing that Nathan is embarrassed and mouths the word, "Busted."

Nathan rolls his eyes and drops his head. Again, the little voice in his head says, "Dumbass."

The five of them head inside and take the elevator up to the top floor to meet the chief in his office.

On the ride up, Ms. Norata is standing behind Nathan and to his right. She is a little shorter than Nathan, so she stands on her tip toes and whispers in his ear, "A black satin and lace thong."

A little shocked Nathan turns his head and whispers, "What?"

Ms. Norata whispers in his ear again, "A black satin and lace thong. You were wondering what I'm wearing under these tight pants weren't you?"

Nathan's face turned red again.

Ms. Norata giggles to herself. She is really enjoying embarrassing Nathan. She can read him like a book.

Nathan is surprised that she is being so aggressive with him considering everything that's happened in the last few weeks.

The elevator reaches the top floor, the doors open and standing right there is Police Chief Tanner.

He holds up his hands and says, “Right on time. Don’t bother stepping off the elevator we need to get going.  I have two police cars waiting downstairs so let’s go.”

He steps onto the elevator, the doors close, and they take it down to the secure underground parking area.  When they step out of the elevator, they see the two police cars waiting for them.

Nathan jumps in the driver’s seat of the first car, Chief Tanner sits in the front passenger seat, and Mr. Bell and Ms. Norata sit in the rear passenger seats.

Mr. Black jumps in the driver’s seat of the second car and Mr. Nagata sits in the front passenger seat.

Nathan and Mr. Black put the cars in gear, step on the gas, drive up the ramp to street level, and turn right on the street in front of the police headquarters.

Nathan touches a button on the touch panel in the dash to turn on the red and blue flashing lights and then changes to the left lane.  Behind him, Mr. Black turns on his red and blue lights and pulls in behind Nathan in the left lane.

They both step on the accelerator pedals and fly past all the cars that have pulled over to the right lane to let them pass.

They arrive at EDF headquarters in no time at all, and after parking the police cars, they head into the building, check in with security, and then take an elevator up to the top floor for their meeting with Admiral Daniels.

Admiral Daniels’ aid meets them at the elevator and guides them to the conference room where the admiral is waiting.  As they enter the conference room, the admiral stands up to greet them.

Chief Tanner shakes the admiral’s hand and says, “Good morning, Admiral.”

“Good Morning, Chief Tanner.”

Nathan shakes the admiral's hand and says, "Good morning, Admiral."

"Good Morning, Captain Stone."

"Thank you all for coming to this meeting, please take a seat. The secretary of the fleet, Admiral Hollister, will be joining us via video conference from Washington D.C. this morning."

Just a few seconds after that, the video screen on the conference room wall changes to display Admiral Hollister sitting at his desk. Everyone in the room stands up to show their respect.

Admiral Hollister says, "Good morning, everyone. Thank you for coming to this meeting and I apologize for the short notice. It was decided this should be a joint meeting since both the EDF and Planetary Police were compromised by the Xandurian infiltrator, and both have been involved in preventing the Xandurians from acquiring the Trynx 3 ore. Admiral Daniels, I turn the floor over to you."

"Thank you, Admiral Hollister. I would like to start by discussing the Xandurian infiltrator. There is no telling how extensive the breach was. We have no way of knowing what she or 'it' told the Xandurians nor can we know what they were able to see and hear through all the surveillance devices 'it' planted. We have completed a sweep of all EDF installations and ships, and the Planetary Police have done the same. At least we know there aren't any more bugs."

Nathan interrupts, "Admiral, we also have no way of knowing if 'it' was the only infiltrator the Xandurians planted. May I suggest before we do anything else, we need to be certain there are no more of them among us? I know it's a huge undertaking, but every person in the government, the EDF and the Planetary Police need to be scanned to make sure they are human."

Admiral Hollister says, "That is a monumental undertaking, Captain Stone. We're talking about hundreds of thousands of people. It's not something that can be done in a few days, we're talking months of scanning. While I agree it needs to be done, we can't wait for the scans to be completed before we move forward. We'll scan the most senior people first and compartmentalize everything accordingly."

Nathan says, "Very well, Admiral."

Admiral Daniels says, "The next thing we need to discuss is the Xandurian time machine. Captain Stone, the Xandurians admitted to you that what we blew up was a decoy, a fake, correct?"

"Yes, Admiral."

"Then we need to find the facility where they are building the real time machine and destroy it. Now how do we do that?"

Nathan says, "I have an idea about that. A number of Xandurian ships were tagged with cloaked tracking devices. Maybe a few of those ships survived. Let's see if we can locate those ships and maybe they will lead us to the facility where the time machine is being built. My tactical officer has access to the EDF's tracking system so when we get back to police headquarters, we'll see what she can find."

Admiral Daniels says, "Excellent idea, Captain Stone. Let me know what you find."

"Thank you, Admiral, I will. There is something else I would like to point out, Admiral Daniels."

"What's that, Captain Stone?"

"Let's say we manage to find and destroy the Xandurian time machine. How long will it be before another alien species builds one and tries to acquire some of the Trynx 3 ore? The ore is the root of the problem. We need to eliminate any possibility of an alien species getting their hands on any of that ore. In my opinion that should be our top priority. Any number of species out there are capable of building a time machine, but if there is nothing to power it, it's just a useless piece of technology and no threat to anyone."

Admiral Hollister leans forward and asks, "So what are you suggesting, Captain Stone?"

"Well, Admiral, I'm suggesting we destroy Trynx 3."

"You want us to destroy an entire planet?"

"Yes sir. It is the only way to be sure. Trynx 3 must be destroyed so this madness can stop."

Everyone in the meeting is quiet for a few moments while they process what Nathan has just said. Destroying a planet is no small thing.

Admiral Daniels is the first to speak, "I agree with Captain Stone. Trynx 3 must be destroyed. It's the only way to be sure that nobody gets their hands on that ore. The question is how do we destroy the planet and guarantee that all the ore is destroyed? We can't just blow up the planet, that would send chunks of the ore hurtling through space for anyone to grab."

Admiral Hollister says, "Sounds like a problem for the EDF's scientific research division to solve."

Admiral Daniels says, "Agreed. I will set up a meeting with their director to discuss the possibilities."

Admiral Hollister says, "Well if there is nothing else, I suggest we bring this meeting to a close and get to work."

Everyone in the room stands up once again to show their respect.

Admiral Hollister says, "Good day, everyone. Hollister out."

The screen shuts down and goes blank. Chief Tanner and Nathan shake Admiral Daniels' hand before he exits the conference room and heads back to his office.

Chief Tanner turns to everyone and says, "Okay, people, let's head back to headquarters."

One by one they file out of the conference room and make their way back to the elevators. They take an elevator down to the lobby, exit the building and walk over to where the police cars are parked.

They get in the cars and start the trip back to police headquarters. Nathan and Mr. Black slowly pull up to and then turn left onto the main street in front of EDF headquarters. They drive back to police headquarters, this time without the flashing red and blue lights.

Fifteen minutes later they are pulling back into police headquarters. After returning the police cars to the secure underground parking area, they head inside and take an elevator up to their offices to get to work on locating those tracking devices.

Ms. Norata sits down at a workstation in the center of their team's bullpen, signs into the terminal, brings up the tracking system.

Ms. Norata says, "This shouldn't take too long."

She activates the holographic projector and displays all active tracking devices of which there are about twenty reporting in total. She then enters a command to display only those trackers that were launched from the Aurora. All the trackers disappear except for four, and all of those are together in one place.

Ms. Norata then enters a command to display the borders of the various species' areas of space. She then zooms the hologram in to display just the Xandurian section of space. All four trackers are together deep in the center of Xandurian space.

Nathan says, "Considering how many of their ships we've destroyed recently, I'll bet my bottom dollar those ships have been pulled back to protect the base where the real time machine is being developed."

Chief Tanner says, "Only one way to find out. I'll contact Admiral Daniels and Admiral Hollister. I'm sure they will want to send a few ships to escort you."

"Very good, Chief, we'll go and prep for takeoff."

"Good luck, Captain."

"Thanks, Chief."

"Okay let's go, people, we have a ship to prep."

Nathan and his crew head to the elevators, take one down to the ground floor and start walking towards the helipad and their ship.

As they approach the front of the ship Nathan says, "Vanessa, unlock and open the lower ramp."

Vanessa's voice comes over the external speakers, "Aye Captain Stone, opening the lower ramp now."

The ramp begins to lower and is fully open by the time Nathan reaches it. Everyone walks up the ramp into the lower bay, Nathan closes the ramp and then everyone heads up to the bridge to prep the ship for takeoff.

A few minutes after everyone has taken their seats on the bridge Vanessa says, "Captain, I have an incoming transmission from Police Chief Tanner."

"On screen, Vanessa."

"Aye Captain."

The main viewing screen powers on and Chief Tanner appears.

"Okay, Captain Stone, I spoke with Admiral Daniels and just as we suspected he wants to send an escort with you. You are to rendezvous with the dreadnought Aurora in orbit. Admiral Anderson is expecting you. Good luck all of you."

"Thank you, Chief. Stone out."

Nathan pushes a button on the command console on his chair to end the transmission and says, "Vanessa, contact Seattle air traffic control and request clearance for takeoff and then contact Earth space flight control and get us clearance for space flight."

"Aye Captain."

"Mr. Bell, fire up the engines."

"Aye Captain."

The crew hears the jet engines as they spin up and start.

Moments later Vanessa says, "Captain, Seattle air traffic control has granted us clearance for a vertical takeoff and Earth space flight control has granted us clearance for space flight. Both report no traffic in the immediate area."

"Thank you, Vanessa."

"Mr. Bell, take us up."

"Aye Captain."

Mr. Bell pushes the throttles half way open, and the ship begins to rise. When the ship reaches two hundred feet, he adjusts the thrust vectoring, and the ship starts to move forward. Mr. Bell rams the throttles wide open after which the ship accelerates and climbs rapidly, pushing the crew back in their seats. Several minutes after takeoff, the sky around the ship turns black as they near the edge of the planet's atmosphere. At this point Mr. Bell disengages the jet engines and closes the air intakes. He then engages the sub-light engines and rams the throttles wide open. The ship accelerates, almost violently, to achieve escape velocity.

Vanessa announces, "Now leaving Earth's gravity. Artificial gravity plating is coming online."

As they break orbit, they can see that that their "escort" comprises approximately half the EDF fleet, not just the Aurora. They can see three dreadnoughts, two battle carriers, about one hundred heavy cruisers, fifty light cruisers and fifty destroyers.

Nathan chuckles and says, "Yup, there's our escort."

Mr. Bell says, "Wow, that's some escort."

"Vanessa, hail Admiral Anderson on the Aurora."

"Aye Captain."

A few moments later Vanessa says, "Captain Stone, I have Admiral Anderson for you."

"On screen, Vanessa."

"Aye Captain."

Admiral Anderson appears on the front view screen.

Nathan smiles and says, "Admiral Anderson, good to see you again, sir. I was told to contact you as soon as we achieved orbit."

"Good to see you again as well, Captain Stone. I'm told this will be about a six-day journey at 14 TSL. You're more than welcome to come aboard the Aurora for the trip if you would like."

"That would be great, thank you, Admiral."

"My pleasure, Captain Stone. You're cleared to land in landing bay alpha, starboard side. You and your crew join me on the bridge after you land."

"Thank you, Admiral, see you soon. Stone out."

"Mr. Bell, you heard the Admiral, head for the Aurora."

"Aye Captain."

Mr. Bell banks the ship and heads for the lead dreadnought. As he approaches the starboard side, he lines the ship up with the huge entrance to landing bay alpha. As he gets closer to the dreadnought, he slows the ship down to almost a slow crawl. Soon the police cruiser passes through the atmospheric force field and into the bay. Once inside, Mr. Bell lowers the landing gear and sets the ship down on the deck. At that point a deckhand steps out in front of the ship with two red flash lights to direct Mr. Bell where to park. Mr. Bell follows his direction into a side bay and then shuts the engines down.

The crew finishes shutting the ship down and then make their way down to the lower bay. They open the ramp and walk down into the Aurora's massive landing bay.

As they walk away from the ship, Nathan says over his shoulder, "Vanessa, close and lock the ramp. Restricted access protocol."

Vanessa's voice comes over the external speakers, "Aye Captain, closing the ramp now. Restricted access protocol enabled."

Nathan and his crew head off across the huge, busy landing bay and over to the internal tram where they board a car and are whisked away at high speed towards the center of the huge dreadnought. When the tram stops, everyone gets off and heads over to a group of elevators. They all get in one elevator and Nathan pushes the button for the bridge. The elevator rises at a substantial speed. The elevator reaches the bridge and the doors open. Nathan and his crew step out of the elevator and onto the bridge. Admiral Anderson turns to look at them and then walks over to greet them.

Admiral Anderson extends his hand to Nathan and says, "Captain Stone, nice to see you again, glad you'll be joining us for this mission. I think you'll be much more comfortable on the Aurora than cooped up in that little police cruiser."

Nathan shakes the admiral's hand and says, "Thank you, Admiral Anderson, it's nice to see you again, sir and thank you for your hospitality."

"My pleasure, Captain Stone. The fleet will get under way shortly. Once we have jumped, why don't I take you and your crew down to the officers' club? The first round is on me."

"That sounds, great Admiral."

The admiral turns and walks to his station at the center of the bridge and says, "Comms, send to all commands in the fleet, tell them to set course for the coordinates of the tracking devices and engage their FTL drives, maximum speed."

"Aye sir."

"Navigator, plot a course to the coordinates of the tracking devices."

"Aye sir, course plotted and laid in."

"Helm, engage the FTL drive and take us up to 14 TSL."

"Aye sir, engaging the FTL drive now."

The huge dreadnought accelerates rapidly away from Earth, and soon the bridge crew sees a bright blue flash of light through the bridge windows as the ship accelerates past the speed of light.

A little more than a minute later the helmsman reports, "Admiral, we have jumped into FTL and have reached 14 TSL. Estimated time to the tracking devices' coordinates is five days twenty-three hours."

"Very well, Helm, steady as she goes."

"Aye sir."

"Tactical, have all the ships of the fleet entered FTL with us?"

The tactical officer runs a quick scan and says, "Aye sir, all ships have entered FTL and have reached 14 TSL. We are the lead ship of the fleet by roughly ten seconds."

"Thank you, Tactical."

Admiral Anderson turns to Nathan and says, "Well, Captain Stone, we have six days until we find out what the Xandurians are up to out there. How about we head down to the officers' club for that drink now?"

"Sounds good to me, Admiral."

The admiral turns back and says, "XO, you have the con."

"Aye sir."

The admiral turns, walks towards the elevator and says, "Okay, everyone, follow me."

Nathan and his crew follow the admiral to the elevator. They get on the elevator and take it down four levels. When the doors open there is another set of doors immediately across the corridor from the elevator. The sign on the wall beside the doors says Officers' Club.

The admiral leads them off the elevator and as he approaches the doors to the officers' club, they slide open automatically.

The room is dimly lit and as they walk in, they see there is a full bar on one side of the room complete with bar stools and a brass foot rail. Behind the bar is a set of cabinets with a stunning display of fancy glass bottles full of alcohol on top of them and each bottle has a different colored light directly underneath it. Spread around the middle of the room are a number of tables and chairs and along the other side of the room are a number of booths that look like they can seat up to eight people each. The front wall of the room consists of several huge windows through which they can see the bow of the ship and the stars streaking past.

Everyone in Nathan's group is impressed with the officers' club. They all served on the battle carrier Invincible, under Nathan, which didn't even have an officers' club let alone one that looked like a night club.

The admiral leads the group over to the booth closest to the front windows so they can watch the stars streak by while they enjoy their drinks and visit.

True to his word, the admiral bought the first round. He also bought the second, third, fourth and fifth rounds. The group was having a lot of fun, sharing stories from past adventures and laughing about some things that happened and things they had seen.

Ms. Norata was sitting across the booth from Nathan and after the third round of drinks, every time Nathan looked at her, she had this lustful, wanting look on her face, like she wanted to absolutely ravage him.

Nathan was unsure if her behavior was exciting him or frightening him. He never realized she was so sexually aggressive. It could be he didn't get to know her well enough before or maybe it was because he and Desiree were together. Now that Desiree is no more…

Several hours later as the group is finishing their eighth round of drinks Nathan says, "Well, we should probably go back to the ship and grab a few things before heading to the guest quarters for the night."

Admiral Anderson says, "Yes, I suppose it is getting late, Captain Stone. Am I correct in assuming you remember what level the guest quarters are on?"

"Yes, I sure do, Admiral. Thank you very much for tonight, I very much enjoyed swapping war stories with you, sir."

"As did I, Captain Stone, as did I."

With that the admiral and Nathan stand up from the booth and shake hands.

Admiral Anderson says, "Goodnight, Captain Stone."

"Goodnight, Admiral."

The admiral turns to Nathan's crew and says, "Goodnight, everyone."

Nathan's crew answers back in unison, "Goodnight, Admiral."

The admiral then heads off towards the elevators.

Nathan says, "Okay, everyone, follow me. We'll head down to the ship, pack a bag and then head to the guest quarters."

Nathan leads his crew out of the officers' club. They take an elevator down to the internal tram and take a tram to the landing bay. They then exit the tram and walk through the still bustling landing bay back to their ship.

When they reach the ship Nathan says, "Vanessa, unlock and open the lower ramp."

Vanessa's voice comes over the external speakers, "Aye Captain Stone, opening the lower ramp now."

When the ramp has finished opening, the crew head up into the lower bay and then up to their private cabins to pack their bags. They each take about twenty minutes to gather their things and then head back down to the lower bay and exit the ship. Mr. Nagata is the first one out, followed by Mr. Bell, then Mr. Black, then Nathan, and finally Ms. Norata.

As they walk away from the ship Nathan once again says over his shoulder, "Vanessa, close and lock the ramp. Restricted access protocol."

Vanessa's voice comes over the external speakers, "Aye Captain, closing the ramp now. Restricted access protocol enabled."

Nathan and his crew head off across the huge landing bay back towards the internal tram. They board a tram and are whisked away at high speed towards the center of the huge dreadnought. When the tram stops, everyone gets off and heads over to a group of elevators. They all get in one elevator and Nathan pushes the button for level forty. The elevator rises at a substantial speed. Soon the elevator arrives at level forty, the doors open and everyone files out and walks down the corridor to the state rooms they stayed in the first time they were aboard the Aurora.

They all go into their respective rooms to get settled in. Nathan looks over at Ms. Norata before entering his room and sees she is giving him that same lustful look she was giving him in the bar. The fact that her room is right next to his registers in his mind as he steps in and the door slides closed behind him.

Nathan isn't tired, so he unpacks his things, and then has a nice long hot shower to relax and wind down. After his shower, he still isn't tired, so he throws on a pair of track pants and a t-shirt and pours himself a generous scotch from the bar. After that he parks himself on the couch, powers on the entertainment unit and browses through the movie library on the holographic display projected from the top of the coffee table. He finds an old science fiction movie from the year 1978, called Battlestar Galactica. He is intrigued by the description and the image of a very large interesting looking spaceship, so he starts it playing.

Nathan turns the volume up about mid-way as the introduction plays and shortly after that there is a knock on his door. Nathan touches the display on the top of the coffee table to pause the movie, gets up and opens the door to find that there is nobody in the corridor outside his quarters.

He says to himself, "That's funny, I swear I heard someone knock on my door."

He closes the door and as it is sliding shut, he hears someone knock a second time. This time he realizes that the knocking is coming from the pass through door that connects his quarters to the quarters next to his, the quarters that are occupied by Ms. Norata. Nathan gets a little adrenaline rush and can feel his heart beating faster. He walks over to the door and opens it.

When it slides open, it reveals Ms. Norata standing there looking very comfortable dressed in some loose fitting white linen pajama bottoms and a loose white t-shirt with a plunging neck line that shows off her cleavage nicely. Nathan gathers she recently got out of the shower as her hair is still damp and it is pulled back in a ponytail. She has reapplied her eye makeup to showcase her beautiful big green eyes. Nathan also notices her perfume and how extremely intoxicating it is.

Ms. Norata can tell that Nathan likes what he sees so with that same seductive little smile she asks, "I'm guessing you can't sleep either?"

Nathan responds with a nervous crackle in his voice, "No, for some reason I'm still wide awake."

Ms. Norata's smile gets a little bigger, "I hope I'm not intruding. I heard you starting a movie. Would you mind some company?"

Nathan steps back and extends his right arm towards the center of his quarters, motioning for her to enter, "No, not at all. Please come in. Make yourself comfortable."

Ms. Norata walks in and sits down on the couch. She looks at the screen and asks, "What are you watching?"

Nathan takes a few steps towards her and the pass through door slides shut behind him.

"I found an old science fiction movie from 1978, called Battlestar Galactica."

Ms. Norata loves big ships with lots of firepower, so she says, "A Battlestar you say? Sounds like it's right up my alley."

Nathan takes a few steps towards the bar and says, "I just poured myself a drink, would you like one before I start the movie?"

"Oh, yes, please."

"The bar is fully stocked, what would you like?"

"How about a vodka martini?"

"Coming right up."

Nathan goes over to the bar and quickly whips up a vodka martini. He walks back over to her and hands her the drink.

"Thank you."

"You're welcome."

Nathan then sits down on the couch beside her and says, "Ready?"

She takes the first sip of her martini and says, "Mmmmm yes, I'm ready."

Nathan touches the display on the top of the coffee table to start the movie playing from the beginning again. Both of them sit back into the couch and get comfortable to watch the movie. After about twenty minutes Ms. Norata reaches forward and touches the display on the coffee table to pause the movie.

She gets up and says, "We need some junk food. You have to have junk food while watching a movie."

Nathan says, "True, but I don't think I have anything."

"That's okay, I have some in my room. I'll go grab it. I'll be right back."

She goes back to her room and is back a minute later with a bag of popcorn and a bag of potato chips.

She looks at Nathan and asks, "Do you have something we could put these in?"

"Let me check the bar."

Nathan gets up, goes over to the bar and looks through all the cabinets. He comes back a few minutes later holding two medium sized bowls.

"I think these will do."

Nathan sits back down on the couch and puts the bowls on the coffee table.

Still standing, Ms. Norata bends over at the waist to pour the popcorn into the first bowl. As she bends over, the front of her t-shirt falls open.

Nathan can't help but stare at her large breasts and the sexy hot pink satin and lace push-up bra that are holding them tight. Nathan can feel his erection growing.

Without straightening up, Ms. Norata pours the potato chips into the second bowl.

Nathan continues to stare at her breasts and her sexy bra. He is also now fully hard, and his erection is pushing upwards on his track pants. It has become very noticeable. Nathan reaches for a throw pillow to put over his lap, but he is too late.

As Ms. Norata finishes pouring the chips into the bowl, she looks at Nathan. She gets a good look before he can cover his erection with the pillow.

Inside she is extremely excited, but on the outside, she decides to play it cool and act like she didn't see anything.

She sits back down next to him, takes a drink of her martini and starts the movie playing again. She leans back into the couch and gets comfortable while she watches Nathan try to be cool about everything out of the corner of her eye.

After a few minutes she turns her head towards Nathan and asks, "Do you like it?"

Nathan looks at her and says, "What? Do I like what?"

"My bra of course, I put it on especially for you."

Nathan is not sure how he should respond. He plays through a few responses in his head, but before he makes a conscious choice, he hears the words, "You did?" come out of his mouth.

Ms. Norata smiles at him and says, "Yes, I did. Would you like a better look at it?"

Nathan's adrenaline has kicked in now and he can feel himself shaking a little from the excitement. He's never stuttered at all before, but he hears himself say, "Y – Y – Y – Yes I would."

Ms. Norata has that look on her face again, like she is going to devour him. She stands up, turns, pulls the throw pillow off Nathan's lap exposing the huge bulge in his track pants and puts one knee on the couch beside Nathan's thigh. She brings her other leg over him and puts her other knee on the couch beside Nathan's other thigh.

After straddling him she sits down on his lap. She can feel his rock hard erection pushing against her. She looks into his eyes and she knows he belongs to her now. She leans back slightly, crosses her arms in front of her, grabbing the bottom of her t-shirt. She then lifts and uncrosses her arms, pulling her t-shirt off over her head.

She throws the t-shirt on the floor and asks, "Well, what do you think?"

Nathan is stunned. Ms. Norata's incredible breasts are mere inches away from his face and the only thing between his mouth and her breasts is one hell of a sexy hot pink push-up bra.

All Nathan manages to eek out is, "Oh my God."

Ms. Norata leans forward and pushes her breasts against Nathan's face. Nathan brings his hands up, grabs her bra covered breasts and squeezes them while rubbing his face against them. Ms. Norata grabs a handful of Nathan's hair and pulls his head back. She lowers her face to his, sticks her tongue into his mouth and kisses him hard.

After a few seconds she breaks the kiss, turns his head to the side, bites his ear lobe and then whispers, "I'm wearing the matching panties too. Why don't you take me into the bedroom, and I'll show them to you as well?"

Nathan is a tall, muscular man and Ms. Norata is a petite, slender woman so he would have no problem standing up and carrying her to the bedroom. As he stands up, she wraps her legs around his waist, sticks her tongue back in his mouth and kisses him hard again. He carries her into the bedroom and puts her down at the foot of the bed.

Ms. Norata grabs his arms and maneuvers the two of them, so Nathan has his back to the bed. She pushes him down on the bed on his back and then takes one step back. She reaches down, unties the drawstring on her pajama bottoms and drops them to the floor.

She wasn't kidding when she said she was wearing the matching panties. She models the sexy, hot pink, satin and lace, string bikini panties for him, spinning around a few times so he can see the back of them as well.

"Well what do you think? Do you like them as well?"

Nathan's mouth and throat were dry, so his voice crackles again as he eeks out, "God yes."

"Good, now stand up and take your shirt off."

Nathan did what he was told. He stood up and took his shirt off exposing his very muscular upper body to her.

Ms. Norata responded by gasping and saying, "Wow."

She let her eyes and her hands explore his body for a minute before grabbing his rock hard erection through his pants with both hands. She is greatly impressed with its size and thickness. She can't wait any longer, so she drops to her knees, hooks her fingers in the waist band of his track pants and pulls them down to his ankles. His large erection springs out and up and is now right in front of her face. She takes it in both hands and engulfs the rest with her mouth. She then removes one of her hands and works more and more of it into her mouth. Soon after she removes her other hand and takes his entire length into her mouth and down her throat.

Nathan gasps out loud as Ms. Norata swallows him whole. Because of his size, no other woman has been able to do that to Nathan before, not even Desiree. He is very impressed with her skill and is amazed how good her warm mouth and throat feels. Ms. Norata pleasures Nathan this way for the next five minutes. Nathan is enjoying what she is doing immensely, but he is looking forward to pleasuring her.

The next time she comes up for air Nathan picks her up, turns and places her on her back on the bed. Nathan then kneels down before her. She knows what he wants, and she wants it too. She pulls her knees up and spreads her legs apart for him. Nathan grabs the edge of her panties, pulls them aside and buries his tongue inside her. Ms. Norata gasps at the intense pleasure. She grabs handfuls of his hair and pulls him into her. Nathan pulls back just a little and finds that special little spot with his tongue. Ms. Norata instantly explodes, a very intense orgasm wracks her body causing her to spasm uncontrollably.

Nathan doesn't give her any time to recover from that intense orgasm. While she was still in orgasm, he stands up between her legs, pulls her panties aside again and drives his large erection deep inside her. Ms. Norata gasps loudly from the sudden intrusion and from Nathan's size. Nathan gives her a few seconds to get used to his size before he slowly pulls almost all the way out and then slowly pushes all the way back inside her.

She grabs the sides of his head with both hands, looks him in the eyes and says, "Nathan hunny, I don't want you to make gentle love to me. I want it hard, rough and fast. The harder the better. Use me for your pleasure in any way you want. Okay?"

Nathan doesn't answer, he just flashes her a devilish grin, pins her arms above her head with one hand, grabs her by the throat with the other hand and rams himself in and out of her as hard and fast as he can. Ms. Norata moans loudly as Nathan absolutely ravages her and within a minute she is up to a full scream as she reaches orgasm again. Nathan continues pounding into her, causing her to experience one long intense orgasm. The excitement is too much for Nathan, he thrusts into her one last time and yells out in pleasure as he explodes deep inside her. He collapses on top of her, exhausted from both the physical activity and a very intense orgasm.

Nathan finally catches his breath and says, "Wow, Ms. Norata, that was incredible."

Still breathing heavy and recovering, Ms. Norata says, "Please, call me Aleena."

"Wow, Aleena, that was incredible."

"Yes, it certainly was. Just so you know that was only the beginning."

Nathan and Aleena spend the next five hours ravaging each other in different ways and in different positions. After completely exhausting each other and collapsing on the bed they both fall into a deep sleep.

In the morning when they wake up Aleena gets out of bed, gathers her things and heads for the door.

Nathan wakes and says, "Where are you off to?"

"Last night was amazing and I look forward to more nights like this, but we just got together. I'm not ready for our other team members to know about us this early in the relationship so for now we'll just keep this between us, act normal and when we go for breakfast we have to emerge from our own quarters."

"I understand perfectly Aleena. See you at breakfast."

Aleena smiles and heads off to her quarters to take a hot shower, Nathan does the same. After which they meet the rest of the team for breakfast and act as if nothing happened at all.

Over the next four nights Aleena dresses in sexy lingerie and surreptitiously enters Nathan's quarters through the pass through door, where they engage in all manner of crazed sexual acts, several of which Nathan had never experienced before. Aleena is almost to the point of being insatiable and Nathan is to the point where all he can think about all day was their next sexual encounter later that night.

On the fifth night, they are attending a formal dinner party with the admiral, so they are all dressed up.

When Nathan arrives at the dinner party, he can't help but admire Aleena. She is dressed in a tight fitting, short, sexy, little, black dress with a plunging neckline and she is wearing very high heels.

She notices that Nathan can't take his eyes off her, so she begins to discreetly tease him. Her teasing goes on all night and has him so worked up that his pent-up sexual energy explodes as soon as he gets back to his quarters and the door slides shut. He can't wait for her to get all sexy for him and come over. He immediately strips naked, opens the door to her quarters, rushes in and grabs her from behind. Aleena lets out a little scream in surprise as he grabs her.

Nathan spins her around to face him and says, "You're going to pay for teasing me all night."

Of course, this did not frighten Aleena, it excited her beyond belief.

Nathan grabs her by the hair and drags her over to one of the armchairs in front of the entertainment system. He pushes her over the back of it, forcing her to bend over, her feet just touching the ground in her high heels. He holds her in place by her hair with the one hand while his free hand pulls her little black dress up over her waist exposing her sexy little black lace bikini panties. He positions his feet inside hers and forces them outward, spreading her legs wide. With his free hand he reaches down and takes a good hold of her panties and tears them off her body with one hard pull. He throws her panties on the floor and then grabs his rock hard erection. He positions himself at her entrance and slams his entire length into her as hard he can.

Aleena lets out a little shriek from the pain of his initial thrust into her. This also causes her to raise her head and shoulders, which makes her back arch, giving Nathan a better angle to pound into her.

Realizing this, Nathan grabs two handfuls of her hair and pulls back towards him causing her back to arch even more. That is when he begins to mercilessly ram himself into her as hard, rough and fast as he can.

Aleena loves being taken by this animal behind her. She begs him, "Oh God, don't stop. Harder. Faster."

After about a minute of being taken like this, she begins to babble incoherently, and Nathan knows she is approaching her first orgasm of the night.

Nathan pounds her through five minutes of one continuous orgasm before ramming into her one last time as he falls over the cliff of an incredibly intense orgasm himself.

When their orgasms subside, they both fall on the floor and lean against the back of the armchair.

Aleena still breathing heavy says, "Wow, you are an absolute animal. I love it."

"Oh, we're not done yet little lady, it's still early."

Aleena smiles and says, "Mmmmm that's what I like to hear. You know, we haven't done it in the shower yet."

Nathan smiles, stands up and offers her his hand to help her stand up. She takes his hand, pulls herself up and then leads Nathan into the bathroom to the shower.

The two sex crazed animals spend an hour ravaging each other in a hot steamy shower and another four hours in Aleena's bed before exhaustion forces them to call it a night and go to sleep. They need to get some sleep tonight, they potentially have a big day tomorrow.

# CHAPTER 9 – NO MORE TIME

The fleet is scheduled to arrive at the coordinates of the tracking devices at approximately 10:30 hours on the morning of the sixth day of their journey.

Nathan and his crew are awake early that morning and after getting ready, all meet in the corridor outside the guest quarters to go for breakfast in the officers' dining room. Nathan and Ms. Norata are the last to come out of their quarters and look very tired. Both are hoping that nobody has put two and two together and figured out their secret. The five of them walk to the elevators and take one down two levels to the officers' dining room. Breakfast is served buffet style so each of them grabs a plate and chooses what they want to eat from a multitude of breakfast foods. They each grab a glass of orange juice and a large coffee and then sit down to eat. During breakfast there is only one topic of conversation, which of course is what they will find when they arrive at the coordinates of the trackers.

Mr. Black was the first to speak, "So, Captain, what do you think we will find when we drop out of FTL?"

"It's difficult to say for sure, but what I'm hoping we find is the science lab where the Xandurians are developing the real time machine. That way we can blow the place straight to hell and be done with the whole time machine mess."

"What if all we find is a few Xandurian ships?"

"Well then we go home, get to work on finding their lab and then go blow it up. I'm hopeful we'll find the lab. If my guess is correct, the Xandurians have pulled all their ships back to protect the real lab and the real time machine."

"That makes sense. Let's keep our fingers crossed."

After breakfast Nathan and his crew go back to the elevators and take one up to the bridge. The fleet is only about an hour away from the coordinates of the tracking devices and Admiral Anderson is already preparing to drop the fleet out of FTL.

As Nathan and his crew walk onto the bridge, they hear Admiral Anderson say, "Comms, open a channel to the fleet."

"Aye sir, channel open."

"Attention all commands, this is Admiral Anderson on the Aurora. We are approximately one hour out. Engage your cloaking devices and rig for silent running. Once your cloaking devices are engaged sound battle stations. Anderson out."

The admiral presses a button on his command console to close the channel.

Everyone on the bridge watches through the port and starboard side bridge windows as the other ships in the battle group fade out and disappear from view.

"Tactical, engage the cloaking device."

The tactical officer answers, "Aye sir, engaging cloaking device now."

"XO, sound battle stations."

"Aye sir."

The XO grabs the microphone and announces over the ship's address system, "Battle stations, battle stations, all hands man your battle stations, this is not a drill."

An alarm sounds after his address and the lights on the bridge change from white to red.

A minute later he says, "Admiral, all sections report battle stations manned and ready."

"Thank you, XO."

The next fifty-five minutes seem to go by slowly on the bridge of the Aurora. Nobody is talking, the ship is ready for battle so there's nothing to do but wait. Everyone is eager and anxious to arrive at the trackers' coordinates, wondering what they will find. After what seemed like an eternity, a series of beeps from the navigator's console signals they are about to arrive at the coordinates of the trackers.

When he hears the beeps Admiral Anderson says, "Comms, we're here. Signal the fleet to drop out of FTL. All stop."

"Aye sir."

"Helm, drop us out of FTL. All stop."

"Aye sir."

Everyone on the bridge sees a bright flash of blue light through the bridge windows as the Aurora drops out of FTL.

Through the bridge windows they see a blue planet off in the distance. The admiral has wisely dropped the fleet out of FTL about five hundred thousand kilometers away from the coordinates of the tracking devices.

"Tactical, activate the main view screen and magnify."

"Aye sir."

The main view screen powers on showing the planet at a distance at first. The tactical officer then zooms in enough to see the planet and what is in orbit of the planet in detail.

The planet seems to be similar to Earth, with a large percentage of water compared to land mass. The planet is not the focus of everyone's interest, however. The focus of interest is the enormous space station orbiting the planet and the two hundred or so war ships that are patrolling around the station and the planet. The space station has a vertical multi-diameter cylinder as its core with four different sized tori mounted at different locations along its length.

The admiral turns and looks at Nathan and says, "If I were a betting man, I would bet every dollar I have that the time machine is being developed somewhere in that station."

"I would agree, Admiral. Why else would they have so many ships protecting it?"

"Well, let's not waste any more time. Helm, move us in closer to the station. About fifty thousand kilometers should do."

"Aye sir."

"Tactical prepare a cloaked drone for launch."

"Aye sir."

It takes the dreadnought about an hour to creep in on the Xandurian space station. Stopping about fifty thousand kilometers away keeps them just outside the patrolling ships perimeter.

"Tactical, launch the drone, let's get a look inside that thing."

"Aye sir, drone launched."

"Switch the main view screen to the video feed from the drone."

"Aye sir."

A few seconds later the main view screen displays the video feed from the drone. Everyone on the bridge watches as the drone heads for the station. The drone is quick so before long it is approaching one of the smaller landing bays on the station. The drone stops just outside the bay and peers inside. The bay appears to be empty at the moment, so the drone slips through the atmospheric force field staying close to the top right corner of the entrance.

After entering, it attaches itself magnetically to the bay wall near the top corner. After that, the drone opens its storage compartment doors and releases hundreds of fly sized micro drones that swarm out and start the monumental task of searching the entire station for the time machine.

Back on the Aurora, Admiral Anderson says, "Okay now we sit and wait to see what they find."

"Helm, we're sitting just outside their ships' patrol radius. If you see a ship getting too close to us, you go ahead and back us off. Don't wait for my order."

"Aye sir."

"Tactical, put the feeds from the micro drones up on the main view screen."

"Aye sir."

The main view screen switches to hundreds of small windows, each showing the video feed from one of the micro drones. Admiral Anderson, Nathan, Ms. Norata, Mr. Bell, Mr. Black and Mr. Nagata all gather close around the huge main view screen so they can see the smaller video feeds up close.

After about an hour of watching the video feeds from the micro drones, a porter shows up with a big carafe of coffee. Everyone pours themselves a large coffee and returns to watching the video feeds.

The Xandurian space station orbiting the planet is huge and could take several days to search. However, after just four and a half hours, one of the fly sized drones makes its way into one of the many science labs, perches itself on a ledge near the ceiling and pans its camera around the room. The video feed from this drone, as luck would have it, is being displayed directly in front of Nathan at head level. He recognizes the shape of the time machine from the fake the special forces team were sent in to destroy.

Nathan yells, "THERE IT IS!"

He reaches out and double taps the small video feed making it expand in size to about four feet across.

The lab looks somewhat similar to the lab found on the asteroid station, but the time machine looks exactly the same as the fake. Just like the fake lab, there are scientists working at computer consoles and on the time machine itself. There are also several armed guards throughout the lab.

Nathan looks at the admiral and says, "Okay, Admiral, we found the time machine now what are we supposed to do about it."

"Well Captain Stone, my orders are to destroy the time machine when we find it. The question is how do we destroy it? These video feeds have been broadcast back to Earth for analysis so I will contact Admiral Hollister to find out what the analysts are recommending we do."

"Comms, get me Admiral Hollister."

"Aye sir."

A few minutes later the communications officer says, "Admiral, I have Admiral Hollister for you."

"On screen."

"Aye sir."

Admiral Hollister appears on the main view screen. He is sitting behind his desk at EDF headquarters. Fleet Admiral Daniels is also on screen standing to the right of Admiral Hollister.

Admiral Hollister is the first to speak, "Admiral Anderson, Captain Stone, excellent work finding the time machine so quickly, gentlemen."

Admiral Anderson and Nathan both answer, "Thank you, Admiral."

Admiral Anderson says, "Now that we have found it, I'm calling to find out what you want me to do about it, Admiral."

"Our analysts started working on a plan of attack the moment we received the video feeds of the space station. It didn't take them long to determine that there was no easy way to destroy that time machine, and quite frankly we're not going to fuck around and put any more lives at risk unnecessarily."

"So, your orders, Admiral Anderson, are to arm and fire a dozen of your mark seven nuclear-tipped missiles and blow that station straight to hell. We realize the Xandurians mean to do us harm should they get their time machine operational, so we feel this response is justified. Wouldn't you agree, gentlemen?"

Nathan is the first to answer, "Absolutely, Admiral."

Admiral Anderson says, "Yes sir. Let's send them and any other species that means to do us harm a message not to fuck with us, sir."

"Very well, Admiral Anderson. You have tactical control. Take whatever precautions you deem necessary and fire when ready."

"Aye sir."

"Good luck gentlemen. Hollister out."

The main view screen switches back to displaying the video feeds from the fly sized drones.

Admiral Anderson says, "Comms, signal the fleet to rendezvous with us at these coordinates and let me know when they have arrived."

"Aye sir."

"Tactical, spin up twelve of the mark seven missiles and target that space station with an even spread. I don't want a single section of that station left intact when we're through."

"Aye sir. Spinning up the missiles and entering a firing solution into the targeting computer now, sir."

"Very well, Tactical, let me know when you have a solution."

"Aye sir."

Time passes slowly on the bridge while waiting for the fleet to arrive and for the tactical officer to produce a firing solution that will guarantee all twelve missiles will avoid the patrolling Xandurian ships and hit the station at virtually the same moment.

The tactical officer has to run several simulations, but after about fifty minutes says, "Admiral, I have a firing solution for you, sir."

"Excellent, thank you, Tactical."

Just then the communications officer says, "Admiral, the fleet has arrived at our coordinates, sir."

"Excellent, thank you Comms."

"Tactical, you may fire when ready."

"Aye sir. Firing in 3... 2... 1... Missiles away."

Everyone on the bridge watches the twelve nuclear missiles appear past the bow of the dreadnought as they break through the ship's cloak and accelerate towards the Xandurian space station. These missiles accelerate rapidly, reaching incredible speeds that allow them to travel the fifty thousand kilometer distance from the dreadnought to the space station in just a few minutes leaving little time for the Xandurians to react before the missiles reach their target.

Admiral Anderson says, "Tactical, put the station on the main view screen and engage the active light dampening on all exterior windows. We don't want anyone blinded by these nukes when they go off."

"Aye sir."

The main view screen switches to display the Xandurian space station and all the bridge windows darken by about seventy-five percent.

Thirty seconds later, the missiles find their mark. Incredible flashes of light followed by massive explosions fill the main view screen. Even with the active light dampeners engaged, enough light gets through to turn the bridge bright white for a few seconds.

When the bright light and the fireballs have cleared, the people on the bridge of the Aurora see that the Xandurian space station has been completely obliterated. As all twelve nuclear missiles were targeted at it, the long central multi-diameter cylinder has pretty much been vaporized. The only thing that remains are small pieces of the cylinder, half the size of the average car back on Earth, sent hurtling out into space in all directions. As for the four different ring sections of the station, only about a quarter of each ring is still visible. The other three quarters of the rings must have been vaporized by the explosions. What remains of the rings is falling back into the atmosphere of the planet and will soon burn up in re-entry.

The shock wave from the explosions and flying debris have decimated close to fifty of the Xandurian warships that were in close proximity to the station. What remains of their broken, burning hulls are tumbling out of control in all directions away from where the space station used to be. Several of them were forced into the planet's atmosphere and burn up on entry.

On the bridge of the Aurora, the crew enjoys a brief celebration over destroying the time machine, the lab it was being developed in and all the scientists involved in the project. Their main mission objective has been completed, however, they know they are not out of the woods yet. They still have a six-day journey back to Earth, and there are still roughly one hundred and fifty Xandurian warships still operational, and they have all started hunting for whoever fired those missiles.

Nathan leans towards Admiral Anderson and asks in a hushed tone, "Are you going to withdraw and jump into FTL before they discover us, or are you going to take out their fleet?"

"We have them outnumber and out-gunned. I don't want to leave a fleet this size intact. Wouldn't you agree, Captain Stone?"

"Absolutely, Admiral. Let's take them out."

The admiral nods at Nathan in agreement, turns towards his tactical officer and says, "Tactical…"

He doesn't get a chance to finish his order. The Xandurians have back tracked where the missiles originated from and have opened fire. The impact of their weapons on the Aurora's shields has revealed its position.

Admiral Anderson finishes his order, "Tactical, disengage the cloaking device and open fire with all forward-facing laser cannons. Fire at will."

"Aye sir."

A majority of the Xandurian ships converge on the Aurora's position and open fire. The instant the cloaking device disengages, and the massive dreadnought becomes visible, the tactical officer pushes the execute button on the targeting computer.

Each of the dreadnought's twenty-four huge forward-facing laser cannon turrets take aim at the Xandurian warships and fire. Each turret has three barrels, and each barrel unleashes an unimaginable amount of energy with each shot. This single dreadnought's laser cannons chew the closest Xandurian ships to bits.

The other two hundred plus ships in the EDF battle group take their lead from the Aurora and disengage their cloaking devices. The fleet has been deployed in an arc formation to maximize the number of laser cannons that can be brought to bear on the enemy ships. The instant their cloaking devices have disengaged, the other ships of the fleet open fire.

The Xandurian ships are no match for the shields and the big guns of the EDF capital ships. Within a few short minutes roughly half of the one hundred and fifty Xandurian ships have been destroyed. The captains of the Xandurian ships realize they are outnumbered and out-gunned but refuse to give up. A dozen of the Xandurians change their tactics and attempt suicide runs at the battle carriers and at a few of the light cruisers.

The dreadnoughts are right next to the battle carriers, so they train all their big guns on the approaching ships. Collectively they blow the Xandurian ships out of the sky before they even get close to the battle carriers.

A couple of the light cruisers weren't so lucky. Two of the Xandurian ships attempting the suicide runs, though heavily damaged, made it through the intense laser cannon barrage and crashed into the main superstructures of the cruisers. The heavily damaged Xandurian ships explode soon after impact and those explosions trigger cascading explosions inside the light cruisers. Less than a minute after impact, the light cruisers are completely obliterated when the cascading explosions reach their main reactors. The resulting fireballs can be seen throughout the fleet.

The big guns of the EDF fleet continue to chew away at the Xandurian ships. Several more attempt suicide runs, but no more get through to cause any damage.

Fifteen minutes after the battle began there are only a handful of Xandurian ships left, the others have all been destroyed.

The commanding officers of the remaining Xandurian ships must have realized that this was a lost cause because they suddenly turn around one hundred and eighty degrees, accelerate away rapidly, and jump into FTL.

Nathan turns to Admiral Anderson, shakes his hand and says, “Congratulations, Admiral.”

“Thank you, Captain Stone. They’ll think twice about challenging us again.”

“Yes sir.”

Admiral Anderson says, “Comms, open a channel to the fleet.”

“Aye sir, channel open.”

“Attention all commands, this is Admiral Anderson on the Aurora. Stand down from battle stations, come about 180 degrees, set course for Earth and engage your FTL drives, maximum speed. Anderson out.”

The admiral presses a button on his command console to close the channel.

“XO, stand down from battle stations.”

“Aye sir.”

The XO grabs the microphone and announces over the ship's address system, "All hands, this is the XO. Stand down from battle stations, repeat stand down from battle stations."

An alarm sounds after his address and the lights on the bridge change from red back to white.

"Navigator, plot a course for Earth."

"Aye sir, course plotted and laid in."

"Helm, bring us about 180 degrees."

Shortly thereafter, the Aurora and all the other ships in the battle group start to turn. When they reach the 180 degree mark, the other ships accelerate away rapidly and disappear in bright blue flashes of light as they jump into FTL.

The last one to jump is the Aurora.

"Helm, engage the FTL drive and take us up to 14 TSL."

"Aye sir, engaging the FTL drive now."

The ship accelerates rapidly and everyone on the bridge sees a bright blue flash of light through the bridge windows as the ship accelerates past the speed of light.

A little more than a minute later the helmsman says, "Admiral, we have jumped into FTL and have reached 14 TSL. Estimated time to Earth is five days twenty-three hours."

"Very well Helm, steady as she goes."

"Aye sir."

## CHAPTER 10 – THE PLAN

Six days later, the fleet arrives home at Earth. Nathan and his crew are preparing to leave the Aurora and head back to Jasper. The Aurora's flight crews have pulled Nathan's police cruiser from its bay and parked it close to the landing bay doors. Nathan's crew has loaded their belongings back on their police cruiser and is on the bridge preparing their ship for takeoff. Everyone except Nathan has already boarded the cruiser. He was just about to walk up the ramp into the ship when he spotted Admiral Anderson walking across the landing bay, presumably to see them off.

As the admiral walks up to Nathan, he extends his hand and says, "I wanted to come down to see you off, Captain Stone."

Nathan shakes his hand and says, "Thank you, Admiral, and thank you for your hospitality."

"It was my pleasure, Captain. Safe flight home."

"Thank you, sir."

The admiral turns and heads off across the landing bay and Nathan heads up the ramp into the cruiser, closing the ramp behind him.

Nathan makes his way up to the bridge and as he is taking his seat says, "Okay, people, it's time to go."

"Vanessa, contact Aurora air traffic control and request clearance for takeoff."

"Aye Captain."

"Mr. Bell, fire up the engines."

"Aye Captain."

The crew hears the jet engines spin up and start.

Shortly after that Vanessa says, "Captain, Aurora air traffic control has cleared us for takeoff."

"Very well, Vanessa."

"Mr. Bell, take her out."

"Aye Captain."

Mr. Bell pushes the throttles forward a little, and the ship begins to rise. When the ship is five feet off the deck, he pulls the landing gear up, rotates the ship one hundred and eighty degrees and then nudges it forward towards the huge bay doors. A few seconds later they pass through the landing bay's atmospheric force field and out into space.

Nathan says, "Vanessa, contact Earth space flight control and get us clearance for re-entry, and then contact Jasper air traffic control, request an approach vector and get us clearance to land on my helipad."

"Aye Captain."

A few minutes later Vanessa says, "Captain, Earth space flight control has granted us clearance for re-entry. Jasper air traffic control has sent us an approach vector and granted us clearance for a vertical landing on your helipad. I have sent the approach vector to Mr. Black's console."

"Thank you, Vanessa."

Mr. Black reviews the data and says, "Confirmed, approach vector laid in, Captain."

"Thank you, Mr. Black."

"Mr. Bell, take us down."

"Aye Captain."

Mr. Bell noses the ship over and begins his descent into the atmosphere. The ship is descending over the Pacific Ocean, heading for the Canadian Rocky Mountains. As they approach Nathan's home in Jasper, Mr. Bell slows the ship down to a crawl and lines it up with the helipad. Soon the ship is hovering at two hundred feet directly over the helipad. Mr. Bell pulls back on the throttles and the ship descends slowly.

When the ship has dropped to fifty feet, the landing gear comes down. A few moments later the wheels touch the ground and Mr. Bell shuts the engines down.

Nathan stands up and says, "Nice smooth landing, Mr. Bell."

"Thank you, Captain."

Just then Vanessa comes on again and says, "Captain, I have an incoming transmission from Fleet Admiral Daniels."

"On screen, Vanessa."

"Aye Captain."

The main view screen activates, and Nathan stands to greet Admiral Daniels.

"Good evening, Admiral Daniels, what can I do for you sir?"

"Good evening, Captain Stone. I wanted to inform you that our scientists have come up with a plan to safely destroy Trynx 3 and its cursed time ore. We have called a meeting for tomorrow morning at 09:00 hours to discuss the plan and I thought you, your crew, and Police Chief Tanner should be a part of that meeting."

"Thank you, sir, we appreciate that and look forward to the meeting."

"Very well, I will see you all at EDF headquarters at 09:00 hours tomorrow. Daniels out."

The main view screen shuts down and then Mr. Bell says, "Wow, I can't wait to hear what they have cooked up for this one."

Nathan says, "Yeah, me too."

Ms. Norata chimes in with, "I'll bet part of the plan will involve cold fusion bombs. Nothing else would be powerful enough to take out an entire planet."

Nathan responds with, "I guess we'll find out tomorrow morning."

The crew finishes shutting down the ship, then heads down to the lower bay, opens the ramp and walks out onto the helipad.

Nathan is the last one out and as he steps off the ramp says, "Vanessa, close and lock the ramp. Restricted access protocol."

Vanessa's voice comes over the external speakers, "Aye Captain, closing the ramp now. Restricted access protocol enabled."

Everyone heads into the house and grabs a beer from the refrigerator in the kitchen on their way in. The last one to come inside, Nathan grabs a beer and heads out onto the deck to start a fire. After he has a good size fire burning in the fire pit, the others bring their beers out and join him on the deck. They sit around the fire and enjoy a couple of beers before discussing what to do about dinner.

Nathan surprises them all by saying, "You know it's been a long time since I've had pizza. Why don't we order some pizzas and just take it easy tonight?"

Nathan is known for eating healthy, so his suggestion of ordering a pizza has caught them all off guard. The four of them have looks of surprise on their faces and look at each other in disbelief.

After a minute of silence Ms. Norata says, "You? You want to order a pizza? Okay who are you and what have you done with Nathan Stone?"

All five of them laugh at Ms. Norata's comment and then Mr. Bell says, "Sounds good, Captain, we could all go for pizza."

After deciding what pizzas they want, Nathan goes inside and orders the pizzas from this little place in Jasper. He then grabs a few more beers and goes back out to sit with his crew by the fire on the deck. About half an hour later a small drone ship appears and hovers over the deck. After a few seconds it descends and lands on the patio table. It then releases its cargo clamps, dropping the thermal box containing the pizzas, and then it lifts off and flies away.

Nathan gets up and says, "Okay everyone, let's eat them while they're hot."

Nathan opens the box, pulls the pizzas out, grabs a big slice of pepperoni and takes his first bite of pizza in years.

Nathan rolls then closes his eyes and says, "Mmmmmmm oh, this is so good."

Mr. Bell says, "Careful there boss, pizza can be habit forming."

They all chuckle and dig into the pizzas. The five of them sit around the fire eating pizza, drinking beer and sharing a few laughs.

Over the course of the evening Nathan notices that every time he looks at Aleena, she has a big smile on her face and the look in her eyes is one of genuine happiness.

Before they know it it's eleven o'clock and time to go to bed. They all have to get up fairly early tomorrow to attend the meeting at EDF headquarters in Seattle. Nathan puts out the fire while the others take care of the pizza boxes and beer bottles. Once everything is cleaned up, they all head off to their rooms to go to sleep.

Nathan brushes his teeth and changes into his pajama bottoms for bed. Just as he is finishing up, there is a quiet knock on his door. He opens it to find Aleena standing there in a pair of pajama shorts and a t-shirt.

She says, "Can I come in for a minute?"

Nathan steps back opening the door and says, "Of course, come in."

After she steps in Nathan closes the door and turns to face her.

She smiles at him and says, "I know it's late and we need to be up early in the morning, but I wanted to stop by and tell you it made me happy to see you smiling and laughing tonight. You haven't done that in a while which is understandable given what's happened recently, but it was really nice to see."

"Thank you, Aleena. I had fun tonight. I know I haven't been myself lately. I am doing better and much of the credit goes to you."

She smiles, leans in, kisses him on the cheek and says, "It's my pleasure, believe me."

Nathan smiles and chuckles.

Aleena walks over to the door, grabs the door knob, turns back to look at Nathan and says, "Goodnight, Nathan. See you bright and early in the morning."

"Goodnight, Aleena, sleep well."

Aleena opens the door and walks out closing the door behind her. Nathan shuts off the lights, climbs into bed and falls asleep, happy for the first time in quite a while.

The next morning everyone is awake at 07:00 hours. After showering and getting dressed they all meet in the kitchen for breakfast at 07:30 hours. They all have coffee and a quick breakfast and then head out to the helipad.

As they approach the front of the ship Nathan says, "Vanessa, unlock and open the lower ramp."

Vanessa's voice comes over the external speakers, "Aye Captain Stone, opening the lower ramp now."

Once open, everyone walks up the ramp into the ship, and then they head up to the bridge. Everyone takes their seats and begin to prep the ship for takeoff.

When ready, Nathan says, "Vanessa, contact Jasper air traffic control and request clearance for takeoff."

"Aye Captain."

"Mr. Black, plot a course for Planetary Police headquarters in Seattle."

"Aye Captain."

"Mr. Bell, fire up the engines."

"Aye Captain."

The crew hears the jet engines spin up and start.

Moments later Vanessa says, "Captain, Jasper air traffic control has granted us clearance for a vertical takeoff, no traffic in the immediate area."

"Thank you, Vanessa."

"Mr. Bell, take us to Seattle."

"Aye Captain."

Mr. Bell pushes the throttles half way open, and the ship begins to rise. When the ship reaches two hundred feet, he adjusts the thrust vectoring, and the ship starts to move forward. Mr. Bell rams the throttles wide open after which the ship accelerates and climbs rapidly, pushing the crew back in their seats. In just a few minutes the ship is up at thirty thousand feet and cruising at five hundred knots.

"Captain, we have reached cruising altitude and speed, we should arrive in Seattle in approximately one hour."

"Thank you, Mr. Bell."

A little over an hour later, as their ship approaches Seattle, Nathan says, "Vanessa, contact Seattle air traffic control and request the approach vector and clearance for a vertical landing at the Planetary Police headquarters helipad."

"Aye Captain."

A few moments later Vanessa says, "Captain, Seattle air traffic control has cleared us for landing at headquarters and has sent me the approach vector. I have sent the approach vector to Mr. Black's console."

"Thank you, Vanessa."

Mr. Black reviews the data and says, “Confirmed, approach vector laid in Captain.”

“Thank you, Mr. Black.”

“Mr. Bell, take us down.”

“Aye Captain.”

Mr. Bell pulls back on the throttles, the ship descends, they break through the clouds and the vast city that is Seattle comes into view. As they approach Planetary Police headquarters, Mr. Bell slows the ship down and banks to port, turning around one hundred and eighty degrees. He slows the ship down to a crawl and lines it up with the helipad. Soon the ship is hovering at two hundred feet directly over the helipad. Mr. Bell pulls back on the throttles a little more and the ship descends slowly. When the ship reaches fifty feet, the landing gear comes down. Moments later the wheels touch the ground and Mr. Bell shuts the engines down.

Nathan stands up and says, “Nice smooth landing Mr. Bell.”

“Thank you, Captain.”

The crew finishes shutting down the ship’s systems, then heads down to the lower bay, opens the ramp and walks out onto the helipad.

Nathan is the last one out and as he steps off the ramp says, “Vanessa, close and lock the ramp. Restricted access protocol.”

Vanessa’s voice comes over the external speakers, “Aye Captain, closing the ramp now. Restricted access protocol enabled.”

Nathan and his crew head inside and take the elevator up to the top floor to meet the chief in his office. The elevator reaches the top floor and the doors open just in time for them to see Police Chief Tanner walk out of the reception area of his office.

He holds up his hands and says, "Perfect timing. I have two police cars waiting downstairs for us so let's go."

He steps onto the elevator, the doors close, and they take it down to the secure underground parking area. When they step out of the elevator, they see the two police cars waiting for them.

Nathan jumps in the driver's seat of the first car, Chief Tanner sits in the front passenger seat and Mr. Bell and Ms. Norata sits in the rear passenger seat. Mr. Black jumps in the driver's seat of the second car and Mr. Nagata sits in the front passenger seat.

Nathan and Mr. Black put the cars in gear, step on the gas, drive up the ramp to street level, and turn right on the street in front of the police headquarters. Nathan touches a button on the touch panel in the dash to turn on the red and blue flashing lights and then changes to the left lane. Behind him Mr. Black turns on his red and blue lights and pulls in behind Nathan in the left lane. They both step on the accelerator pedals and fly past all the cars that have pulled over to the right lane to let them pass.

They arrive at EDF headquarters in no time at all and after parking the police cars and checking in through security, they head up to the top floor to meet with Admiral Daniels.

Admiral Daniels' aid meets them at the elevator and guides them to the conference room where the admiral is waiting. As they enter the conference room, the admiral stands up to greet them.

Chief Tanner shakes the admiral's hand and says, "Good morning, Admiral."

"Good Morning, Chief Tanner."

Nathan shakes the admiral's hand and says, "Good morning, Admiral."

"Good Morning, Captain Stone."

The admiral says, "Thank you all for coming to this meeting, please take a seat. The secretary of the fleet, Admiral Hollister, will be joining us via video conference from Washington D.C. this morning."

A few seconds later, the video screen on the conference room wall changes to display Admiral Hollister sitting at his desk. Everyone in the room stands up to show their respect.

Admiral Hollister says, "Good morning, everyone. Thank you for coming to this meeting, and I apologize for the short notice. It was decided this should be a joint meeting since both the EDF and Planetary Police have been heavily involved in this whole Trynx 3 mess that both should take part in putting an end to this madness once and for all."

Chief Tanner says, "Thank you, Admiral Hollister, we appreciate you including us."

"Of course, Chief Tanner. Now I will turn the meeting over to Admiral Daniels to explain the solution our scientists have come up with."

Admiral Daniels says, "Thank you, Admiral Hollister."

The admiral activates the holographic projector at the center of the conference room table. It starts up and projects a 3D picture of Trynx 3 with the base on the surface, the defensive satellites in orbit and the space station.

"Here you see Trynx 3, the biggest pain in our collective asses for the past few years. As you know we tasked our scientists with destroying the planet without blowing chunks of the time ore out into space in all directions and they have come up with a plan to do just that. The plan has three major components to it. The first, and most obvious phase, will be to remove all in place defenses and evacuate the planet."

The admiral presses a button on the control console to remove the base, the satellites and the space station from the projection.

He then continues, "The second phase will be to deploy a new web of satellites in a high orbit surrounding the planet. These satellites will be fitted with modified shield generators that will disintegrate anything that comes in contact with them."

The admiral presses another button on his console that adds the web of satellites around the planet.

"The third, and final phase of this plan, consists of loading thirty-six high yield cold fusion warheads into thirty-six individual self-propelled tunneling machines. These machines will tunnel down almost to the core of Trynx 3 spaced out in ten degree intervals."

The admiral presses another button on his console that adds the tunneling machines and shows them burrowing into the planet.

After hearing and seeing this, Ms. Norata looks across the conference room table and mouths the words, "I told you so," to Nathan, Mr. Bell and Mr. Black.

All three of them smile back at her and Nathan shakes his head.

The admiral continues, "Once the satellites are powered up, and the tunneling machines have burrowed to the proper depth, we will set off the cold fusion bombs. Our scientists estimate that ninety percent of the planet will be vaporized to particles no bigger than a grain of sand by the force of the explosions. The other ten percent will be chunks no bigger than a child's soccer ball. The orbiting satellites will disintegrate any ejected debris that escapes the initial blast. Just for added peace of mind the satellites will also scan outwards to make sure that nothing escapes."

The admiral presses another button on his console that plays the animated destruction sequence of the planet.

The admiral finishes by saying, "Not one single small pebble of the time ore will be allowed to escape. We will make sure that every molecule of that ore is destroyed."

Nathan says, "Admiral what about the shock wave from the explosions? Won't it knock the satellites out of position?"

"Excellent question, Captain Stone. The satellites will link together to form one large shield around the planet. Our scientist's calculations show that the shield will be strong enough to protect the satellites from the shock wave allowing them to disintegrate anything that survives the blast. Questions anyone?"

Mr. Bell says, "Yes, Admiral. How long will it take to put this plan into operation and destroy the planet?"

"Another excellent question. The timeline I've been given is thirty days until we can destroy Trynx 3. Twenty-one days to modify the shield generators, get them installed on the satellites and get the cold fusion bombs fitted into the tunneling machines. Then we have to ship everything out to Trynx 3. It will take the next eight days to get the satellites deployed and get the tunneling machines to bore into position near the planet's core. After that we clear everybody out and press the button. BOOM no more Trynx 3, no more time ore, no more problems."

Nathan says, "Admiral, can my crew and I be present at the time of detonation? Trynx 3 has been a pain in our ass for a long time now so we'll be happy to see it go away. That and it's not every day you get to see a planet explode."

"Yes, of course, Captain Stone. I'll make the arrangements for you to view the detonation from the Aurora. You're right, it's not every day you get to see a planet explode. Admiral Hollister and I will join you on the Aurora to see the fireworks."

"Thank you, Admiral Daniels, Admiral Hollister."

"My pleasure, Captain Stone. Any other questions?"

Everyone at the table shakes their heads, so the admiral says, "All right then, I will see you all on the Aurora in about a month."

Everyone in the room stands up once again to show their respect.

Admiral Hollister says, "Yes, see you on the Aurora in a month. Good day, everyone. Hollister out."

The screen shuts down and goes blank. Chief Tanner and Nathan shake Admiral Daniels' hand before he exits the conference room and heads back to his office.

Chief Tanner turns to everyone and says, "Okay people, let's head back to headquarters."

One by one they file out of the conference room and make their way back to the elevators. They take an elevator down to the lobby, exit the building and walk over to where the police cars are parked. They get in the cars and start the trip back to police headquarters. Nathan and Mr. Black slowly pull up to and then turn left onto the main street in front of EDF headquarters. They drive back to police headquarters, this time without the flashing red and blue lights.

Nathan asks Chief Tanner, "How are the scans coming along?"

"We have finished our scans. Every member of the police force and all the support staff were scanned. No other cybernetic organisms were found. Last report I saw from the EDF they were fifty percent finished their scans and haven't found any others either. Looks like Ms. Arnoult just may have been the only one."

Not really sure how to feel about that Nathan says, "Well that's a good bit of news I guess."

"Look, Nathan, don't beat yourself up over it. She or rather 'it' had us all fooled. It's not your fault."

"I suppose so, but she was on my team and she was in my bed. I was the closest to her. If anyone should have picked up on something it should have been me. This was very personal to me."

“I understand how you feel, but you have to realize and accept that their technology was just that good. She fooled everyone and didn’t slip once in more than two years.”

“That’s true, but I hate being made a fool of. At any rate I can’t wait for next month when they blow Trynx 3 away. If all goes according to plan this particular problem will just go away.”

“Yes, that will be a good day indeed.”

Soon they arrive back at police headquarters and have parked the police cars back in the secure underground parking area.

As they are about to get out of the car the chief says, “Let’s get back to work, and before we know it, Trynx 3 will be a cloud of dust and our lives will be back to normal. What do you say we head upstairs and go catch some bad guys?”

Nathan says, “Sounds good to me, Chief.”

“All right then.”

Chief Tanner, Nathan and his crew head over to the elevators and head up to their respective offices.

Nathan pulls open the new case files, chooses a case from the list and reviews it before he briefs his crew. Chief Tanner was right, it’s good to get back to normal police work.

# CHAPTER 11 – GOOD BYE TRYNX 3

Thirty days goes by quickly as Nathan and his crew have been busy solving case after case, flying all over Earth's space tracking down and locking up bad people and bad aliens.

This morning as Nathan and his crew land on the helipad at Planetary Police headquarters, Vanessa comes on and says, "Captain Stone, I have an incoming transmission from Police Chief Tanner."

"On screen, Vanessa."

"Aye Captain."

The main view screen activates displaying Chief Tanner sitting at his desk in his office on the top floor of police headquarters.

Nathan says, "Good morning, Chief Tanner. We just landed on the helipad."

"Good morning, Captain Stone. Yes, I know, I wanted to catch you before you left your cruiser."

"What can I do for you, Chief?"

"I was hoping you could give me a ride."

"Chief?"

"It's time, Captain Stone. The Aurora just arrived in orbit. They're waiting for us."

Nathan smiles and says, "Yes, sir, Chief, it would be my pleasure to give you a ride up to the Aurora."

"Very good, Captain Stone, I'll be down in five minutes. Tanner out."

The transmission cuts off and Nathan says, "Mr. Bell, don't bother shutting down the engines. Apparently, we're leaving again."

Mr. Bell turns and smiles at Nathan and says, "Aye Captain."

Nathan gets up and says, "I'm going to go meet the chief on the helipad. I'll be back shortly."

Nathan exits the bridge and makes his way down to the lower bay. He opens the ramp, walks down and steps out onto the helipad. There he waits, standing with his hands clasped behind his back until the chief arrives.

Nathan turns and extends his left arm towards the open ramp and says, "After you, Chief."

"Thank you, Captain Stone."

The two of them walk up the ramp into the lower bay of the cruiser. Nathan closes the ramp and says, "If you'll follow me, Chief, I will guide you up to the bridge."

"Lead on, Captain Stone."

The two of them make their way up to the bridge. Nathan enters the bridge first followed by Chief Tanner. The crew stands up to greet the chief.

Chief Tanner says, "Good morning, everyone. Please be seated."

Nathan extends his right arm towards his chair and says, "You can have my seat, Chief."

Chief Tanner says, "Thank you, Captain Stone," and then walks over and takes a seat.

"All right people, let's get going. We have a dreadnought to catch."

"Vanessa, contact Seattle air traffic control and request clearance for takeoff and then contact Earth space flight control and get us clearance for space flight."

"Aye Captain."

Moments later Vanessa says, "Captain, Seattle air traffic control has granted us clearance for a vertical takeoff and

Earth space flight control has granted us clearance for space flight. Both report no traffic in the immediate area."

"Thank you, Vanessa."

"Okay Mr. Bell, take us up."

"Aye Captain."

Mr. Bell pushes the throttles half way open and the ship begins to rise. When the ship reaches two hundred feet, he adjusts the thrust vectoring and the ship starts to move forward. Nathan is standing behind Chief Tanner holding on to the bulkhead above. Keeping this in mind, Mr. Bell accelerates and climbs more gradually instead of ramming the throttles wide open. Several minutes after takeoff, the sky around the ship turns black as they near the edge of the planet's atmosphere. At this point Mr. Bell disengages the jet engines and closes the air intakes. He then engages the sub-light engines and pushes the throttles up. The ship accelerates and soon achieves escape velocity.

Vanessa announces, "Now leaving Earth's gravity. Artificial gravity plating is coming online."

As they break orbit, Mr. Black says, "Captain, I have the Aurora bearing two seven five degrees at a distance of forty-five thousand kilometers."

"Very well, Mr. Black."

"Mr. Bell, change course bearing two seven five degrees. Take us to the Aurora."

"Aye Captain."

Mr. Bell banks the ship and the Aurora appears in the front bridge windows. Even from this distance the dreadnought appears to be massive.

Chief Tanner says, "Oh my God that's a huge ship."

Nathan replies, "If you think it looks huge from here, just wait until we get close to it."

As they get closer Nathan says, "Vanessa, contact Aurora air traffic control and request clearance to land in landing bay alpha."

"Aye Captain."

A minute later Vanessa says, "Captain, Aurora air traffic control says clearance to land in landing bay alpha, port side is granted."

"All right, Mr. Bell, take us in."

"Aye Captain."

When they are about two kilometers away from the dreadnought Chief Tanner gets up and walks right up to the bridge windows. He scans from one side to the other in amazement over the sheer size of the Aurora.

"I can't believe how big this ship is. That thing is massive."

Nathan says, "I felt the same way when I first laid eyes on her and that's coming from someone who spent five years on the bridge of a battle carrier."

As they approach, Mr. Bell lines the ship up with the huge entrance to landing bay alpha. As he gets closer to the dreadnought, he slows the ship down to almost a slow crawl. Soon the police cruiser passes through the atmospheric force field and into the bay. Once inside, Mr. Bell lowers the landing gear and sets the ship down on the deck. At that point a deckhand steps out in front of the ship with two red flash lights to direct Mr. Bell where to park. Mr. Bell follows his direction into a side bay and then shuts the engines down.

The crew finishes shutting the ship down and then make their way down to the lower bay. They open the ramp and walk down into the Aurora's massive landing bay.

As they walk away from the ship Nathan says over his shoulder, "Vanessa, close and lock the ramp. Restricted access protocol."

Vanessa's voice comes over the external speakers, "Aye Captain, closing the ramp now. Restricted access protocol enabled."

Nathan leads Chief Tanner and his crew across the huge landing bay to the internal tram where they board a tram and are whisked away at high speed towards the center of the immense dreadnought. When the tram stops, everyone gets off and heads over to a group of elevators. They all get in one elevator and Nathan pushes the button that says bridge on it. The elevator rises at a substantial speed. The elevator reaches the bridge and the doors open. Nathan and his crew step out of the elevator and onto the bridge. Admiral Anderson turns to look at them and then walks over to greet them.

Admiral Anderson extends his hand to Chief Tanner and says, "Chief Tanner, so nice to meet you in person, sir. I'm glad you're joining us for this mission."

"Thank you, Admiral Anderson, nice to meet you in person as well and thank you for letting us hitch a ride with you."

"Oh, it's my pleasure, sir."

Admiral Anderson turns to Nathan, extends his hand and says, "Captain Stone, always a pleasure to see you."

Nathan shakes the admiral's hand and says, "Thank you, Admiral Anderson, it's nice to see you again, sir."

Admiral Anderson addresses them all, "We will be getting under way shortly, we're just waiting for two more guests to arrive. Admiral Hollister and Admiral Daniels' transport should be landing any minute now so if you will excuse me, I'm going to head down to the landing bay to greet them and escort them back up to the bridge."

With that, Admiral Anderson walks over to the elevator and steps on. The doors close and he is whisked away.

Chief Tanner says, "I have to go and look out those front windows."

He, Nathan and Nathan's crew walk over to the front bridge windows and look out at the bow of the ship.

Chief Tanner says, "I can't get over how massive this ship is."

Nathan says, "Yes, she and her five sister ships are a wonder to behold that's for sure. I don't know of any species in our galaxy that could stand up to the EDF fleet. Nobody else has ships this big and weapons like these, let alone the sheer number of ships we have."

They all stand at the windows staring out in amazement for the next ten minutes until Admiral Anderson arrives back on the bridge with Admiral Daniels and Admiral Hollister in tow.

When Admiral Anderson steps out onto the bridge, the ship's computer announces, in its female voice, "Admiral on the bridge."

The entire bridge crew stands and snaps to attention to greet and show respect to all three admirals present today.

Admiral Anderson says, "At ease, everyone."

Chief Tanner and Nathan walk over to greet the two admirals.

Chief Tanner shakes Admiral Daniels' hand and says, "Admiral Daniels, it's nice to see you again, sir."

"Thank you, Chief Tanner, it's nice to see you again as well."

Chief Tanner then turns to Admiral Hollister, shakes his hand and says, "Admiral Hollister, it's a pleasure to finally meet you in person, sir."

"The pleasure is all mine, Chief Tanner, I'm glad you could join us this morning."

"Thank you for inviting us, I wouldn't miss this for the world."

Nathan then steps up, shakes both of their hands and says, "Admiral Daniels, Admiral Hollister, nice to see you again."

Admiral Daniels says, "Captain Stone, nice to see you again."

Admiral Hollister says, “Yes, Captain Stone, always a pleasure.”

With the formalities out of the way Admiral Anderson says, “Well, we better get under way.”

“Navigator, plot a course for Trynx 3.”

“Aye sir, course plotted and laid in.”

“Helm, engage the FTL drive and take us up to 14 TSL.”

“Aye sir, engaging the FTL drive now.”

The huge dreadnought accelerates rapidly away from Earth and everyone on the bridge sees a bright blue flash of light through the bridge windows as the ship accelerates past the speed of light.

A little more than a minute later the helmsman reports, “Admiral, we have jumped into FTL and have reached 14 TSL. Estimated time to Trynx 3 is six hours.”

“Very well, Helm, steady as she goes.”

“Aye sir.”

“XO, you have the bridge.”

“Aye sir.”

Admiral Anderson turns to his guests and says, “Now that we’re under way, why don’t we all head down to my private dining room and have brunch?”

Admiral Hollister says, “Excellent idea, Admiral, I’m famished.”

Admiral Daniels agrees, “Yes, excellent idea. I didn’t have time for breakfast this morning.”

Admiral Anderson says, “Well then just follow me, everyone,” and then leads the whole group over to the elevator. They take the elevator down two levels and then he leads them to his private dining room.

When they enter the dining room, they see a good sized table in the center of the room with about sixteen chairs around it and a buffet table off to the right side that is just loaded with all sorts of breakfast foods.

As everyone walks in Admiral Anderson extends his right arm and says, “Please, everyone, dig in.”

The group spends the next two hours eating and visiting, sharing old war stories and discussing the pending destruction of Trynx 3. Admiral Anderson offers to take the group on a guided tour of some of the more interesting sections of the Aurora. There is a lot to see on such a big ship, so the tour ends up being about three hours long and takes them through areas such as engineering where they saw the massive thruster engines, the FTL drive, the reactors that power the ship, the shield generators and the cloaking device. They also get a tour of some of the tactical systems such as the missile launch bays and one of the massive laser cannon turrets. Other areas they visit include the state-of-the-art medical bay, one of the many mess halls, one of the entertainment areas and the huge glass observation deck at the very top of the main superstructure, just above the bridge. The observation deck is a large glass hemisphere that allows a three hundred and sixty degree view of space and has several large telescopes for those that want to have a closer look at something they spot out in the cosmos.

The group spends the next hour in the observation deck watching the stars streak past and looking at various cosmic phenomena through the telescopes. They are all mesmerized by what they are seeing. The only thing more amazing than standing in a big glass bubble out in space is standing on the edge of the flight deck of a battle carrier in space with no space suit on with nothing but an invisible force field between you and oblivion.

While the group is on the observation deck, the Aurora drops out of FTL and arrives at Trynx 3. To those on the observation deck it appeared as if the stars going past slowed down, there was a bright blue flash of light and then Trynx 3 and the EDF fleet instantly appeared.

Admiral Anderson says, “Well, we have arrived at Trynx 3 so let’s head back down to the bridge now.”

He leads them from the observation deck down one flight of stairs to the elevator. They take the elevator down one level to the bridge.

When Admiral Anderson steps out onto the bridge, the ship’s computer announces, in its female voice, “Admiral on the bridge.”

Once again, the entire bridge crew stands and snaps to attention.

Admiral Anderson says, “At ease, everyone.”

The bridge crew takes their seats again and goes back to doing their jobs.

Nathan walks over to the front bridge windows and looks out at Trynx 3. He notices that the orbiting military space station has been removed, presumably being towed to Earth or one of her colonies. He sees that about half of the EDF fleet is still present, though they have pulled back quite a way away from the planet. He also sees the defensive satellites have been removed and replaced by a huge web of different satellites, presumably the ones mentioned in the briefing a month ago with the modified shield generators that will disintegrate any remnants ejected into space after the explosion.

The Aurora’s communications officer says, “Excuse me, Admiral Anderson, I have a message for you from the demolition team’s leader. He says everything is ready, the cold fusion bombs have all tunneled to the required depth, the satellites are in place and powered up, the planet has been completely evacuated, and the fleet has pulled back to a safe distance. He’s just waiting for your okay to arm and detonate the cold fusion bombs.”

“Thank you, Comms.”

"Helm, come about and rendezvous with the rest of the fleet at the specified safe distance."

"Aye sir."

The huge dreadnought turns to starboard and heads towards the fleet. The helmsman pilots the ship past the fleet, performs a tight one hundred and eighty degree turn and brings the dreadnought to a full stop underneath the fleet, just slightly out in front.

The helmsman says, "We're in position, Admiral."

"Very well, Helm."

"Comms, open a channel to the fleet."

"Aye sir, channel open."

"Attention all commands, this is Admiral Anderson on the Aurora. Raise your shields, full power in reflective mode and engage the active light dampening on all exterior windows. We don't want anyone blinded when these cold fusion bombs go off. Anderson out."

The admiral presses a button on his command console to close the channel.

"Tactical, raise our shields, full power in reflective mode."

"Aye sir, shields are up."

"Tactical, put Trynx 3 on the main view screen and engage the active light dampening on all exterior windows."

"Aye sir."

The main view screen switches to display Trynx 3 and all the bridge windows darken by about seventy-five percent.

Admiral Anderson turns to Admiral Hollister and says, "Admiral Hollister, we are in position, do I have your permission to tell the demo team leader to arm and detonate the bombs, sir?"

"You have my permission, Admiral Anderson, proceed."

"Thank you, sir."

He then turns back and says, "Comms, get me the demo team leader and put him on the speakers."

"Aye sir, I have him on the speakers for you now, sir."

The demo team leader says, "Admiral, this is Captain Robert Wallace, I am the demolition team's leader. Do I have your permission to arm and detonate the bombs, sir?"

"Captain Wallace, this is Admiral Anderson. You have my permission to arm and detonate the bombs. You have a green light, Captain."

"Thank you, sir. I have armed the bombs. Beginning the ten second count down. 10... 9... 8... 7... 6... 5... 4... 3... 2... 1... Detonating now."

Two seconds later the entire planet explodes and disappears in a bright flash of white light and a huge fireball. A good deal of the flash was cut down by the active light dampening, it was still very bright, but not bright enough to damage peoples' eyes. A few seconds after the main explosion, the shock wave slams into the shield projected from the web of satellites deployed around the planet. The shield absorbs the energy from the shock wave and totally negates its force. A few seconds after the shock wave dissipates, small chunks of the planet begin slamming into the shield, but again the shield does the job it was designed to do and disintegrates anything that touches it.

After about ten minutes the dust cloud has cleared away enough to see that the entire planet is gone and with it went the danger of any alien species getting their hands on the time ore. The only thing that is left is a cloud of dust particles no bigger than a grain of sand.

Everyone on the bridge of the Aurora cheers and applauds at the successful destruction of the planet.

Admiral Anderson says, "Captain Wallace, great job. Really well done."

"Thank you, sir."

The admiral says, "Anderson out," and then presses a button on his command console to close the channel.

The three admirals and Nathan all shake each other's hands for a job well done.

Admiral Hollister says, "Thank God that's over with, I think we can all relax just a bit more."

Admiral Daniels says, "Absolutely, sir. Good bye Trynx 3."

Nathan adds, "And good riddance."

Admiral Anderson says, "Just a little cleanup work to do now. Most of the fleet will come home with us. A few ships will stay here for about another week to dismantle and retrieve the web of satellites before returning home."

Admiral Anderson says, "Comms, open a channel to the fleet."

"Aye sir, channel open."

"Attention all commands, this is Admiral Anderson on the Aurora. Set course for Earth and engage your FTL drives, maximum speed. Anderson out."

The admiral presses a button on his command console to close the channel.

"Navigator, plot a course for Earth."

"Aye sir, course plotted and laid in."

One by one the other ships in the fleet accelerate away rapidly and disappear in bright blue flashes of light as they jump into FTL.

As usual, the last one to jump is the Aurora.

Admiral Anderson says, "Helm, engage the FTL drive and take us up to 14 TSL."

"Aye sir. Engaging the FTL drive now."

The ship accelerates rapidly and everyone on the bridge sees a bright blue flash of light through the bridge windows as the ship accelerates past the speed of light.

A little more than a minute later the helmsman says, "Admiral, we have jumped into FTL and have reached 14 TSL. Estimated time to Earth is six hours."

"Very well, Helm, steady as she goes."

"Aye sir."

Admiral Anderson turns to face Admiral Hollister, Admiral Daniels, Nathan and his crew and says, "Shall we head down to the officer's club and celebrate with a drink?"

Admiral Hollister says, "Excellent idea, Admiral Anderson."

Admiral Anderson leads everyone to the elevators and takes them down to the officer's club. They spend the next few hours celebrating the destruction of Trynx 3 and the elimination of the troublesome time ore.

Everyone is still sitting in the officers' club when the fleet arrives back at Earth. Through the windows they see a bright blue flash of light and then the Earth suddenly appears past the bow of the massive ship.

Admiral Anderson says, "Ah, we're home again. I'm sure you're all eager to get back so if you follow me, I will escort you all down to the landing bay."

Admiral Anderson leads everyone over to the elevators. They step into an elevator and take it down to the level that the landing bays are on. They board the tram and are whisked away at high speed. When they reach the landing bay they step off the tram and Admiral Anderson leads them over to Admiral Hollister's and Admiral Daniels' transport.

Admiral Anderson salutes them, shakes both of their hands and says, "Admiral Hollister, Admiral Daniels, it was an honor to have you aboard. Safe journey home."

Admiral Hollister says, "Thank you for having us aboard this amazing ship, Admiral."

Admiral Daniels says, "Yes, thank you for having us aboard. She is an incredible ship, Admiral."

"Thank you, sirs."

Admiral Hollister turns and shakes Nathan's and Chief Tanner's hands and says, "Captain Stone, always a pleasure to see you. Chief Tanner, a pleasure meeting you, sir."

Nathan says, "Always a pleasure to see you too, Admiral."

Chief Tanner says, "A pleasure to meet you as well, Admiral. Have a safe flight, sir."

Admiral Daniels smiles, shakes Nathan's hand and says, "You know, Captain Stone, we're building a few more dreadnoughts. You'd look pretty good standing on the bridge of one of them. Or even better yet one of the second generation battle carriers we're building. Just say the word and one of them will be yours. Admiral Stone has a much better ring to it than Captain Stone, don't you think?"

Nathan smiles and says, "Thank you for the offer, Admiral, but I'm happy with the Planetary Police."

"Very well, Captain, if anything changes in that respect just let me know. I can have you on the bridge of a dreadnought or a new battle carrier in less than a day."

"I will, sir, thank you, Admiral."

"All right, take care, Captain."

"You too, Admiral."

Admiral Daniels turns and shakes Chief Tanner's hand and says, "Chief Tanner, a pleasure, sir. Take care."

"The pleasure was mine, Admiral. Have a safe flight, sir."

The admirals turn and walk up the ramp into their transport. The ramp closes behind them and the engines fire up. Shortly thereafter the engines throttle up, the transport lifts off the deck, turns one hundred and eighty degrees and heads out the huge bay doors, through the atmospheric force field and out into space. After exiting the bay, it turns ninety degrees to starboard and disappears from view.

Admiral Anderson then escorts Chief Tanner, Nathan and his crew over to their police cruiser. The Aurora's flight crews have pulled it from its bay and parked it close to the landing bay doors.

As they approach the front of the ship Nathan says, "Vanessa, unlock and open the lower ramp."

Vanessa's voice comes over the external speakers, "Aye Captain Stone, opening the lower ramp now."

Nathan turns and shakes Admiral Anderson's hand and says, "Thank you for having us aboard, Admiral."

"It was my pleasure, Captain. Safe flight home."

"Thank you, sir."

Admiral Anderson turns to Chief Tanner, shakes his hand and says, "Chief Tanner, a pleasure, sir. Take care."

"The pleasure was mine, Admiral. Thank you for having us aboard, sir."

The admiral turns and heads off across the landing bay and Chief Tanner, Nathan and his crew head up the ramp into the cruiser, closing the ramp behind them. They all make their way up to the bridge and take their seats.

As before Nathan offers his chair to Chief Tanner and says, "Okay, people, it's time to go."

"Vanessa, contact Aurora air traffic control and request clearance for takeoff."

"Aye Captain."

"Mr. Bell, fire up the engines."

"Aye Captain."

The crew hears the jet engines spin up and start.

Shortly after that Vanessa says, "Captain, Aurora air traffic control has cleared us for takeoff."

"Thank you, Vanessa."

"Mr. Bell, take her out."

"Aye Captain."

Mr. Bell pushes the throttles forward a little and the ship begins to rise. When the ship is five feet off the deck, he pulls the landing gear up, rotates the ship one hundred and eighty degrees and then nudges it forward towards the huge bay doors. A few seconds later they pass through the landing bay's atmospheric force field and out into space.

Nathan looks at Chief Tanner and says, "Chief, we're going to celebrate with a few beers around a nice fire, would you care to join us?"

Chief Tanner smiles and says, "Yes, I would like that very much, Captain Stone."

"Excellent, sir."

"Vanessa, contact Earth space flight control and get us clearance for re-entry and then contact Jasper air traffic control, request an approach vector and get us clearance to land on my helipad."

"Aye Captain."

A few minutes later Vanessa says, "Captain, Earth space flight control has granted us clearance for re-entry. Jasper air traffic control has sent us an approach vector and granted us clearance for a vertical landing on your helipad. I have sent the approach vector to Mr. Black's console."

"Thank you, Vanessa."

Mr. Black reviews the data and says, "Confirmed, approach vector laid in, Captain."

"Thank you, Mr. Black."

"Mr. Bell, take us down."

"Aye Captain."

Mr. Bell noses the ship over and begins his descent into the atmosphere. The ship is descending over the Pacific Ocean, heading for the Canadian Rocky Mountains. As they approach Nathan's home in Jasper, Mr. Bell slows the ship down to a crawl and lines it up with the helipad. Soon the ship is hovering at two hundred feet directly over the helipad. Mr. Bell pulls back on the throttles and the ship descends slowly. When the ship has dropped to fifty feet, the landing gear comes down. A few moments later the wheels touch the ground and Mr. Bell shuts the engines down.

Nathan stands up and says, "Nice smooth landing, Mr. Bell."

"Thank you, Captain."

The crew finishes shutting down the ship's systems, then everyone heads down to the lower bay, opens the ramp and walks out onto the helipad.

Nathan is the last one out and as he steps off the ramp says, "Vanessa, close and lock the ramp. Restricted access protocol."

Vanessa's voice comes over the external speakers, "Aye Captain, closing the ramp now. Restricted access protocol enabled."

The six of them head into the house. One by one they grab a beer from the refrigerator and then take a seat on the deck.

Nathan holds his beer up and says, "To Trynx 3, good bye and good riddance."

They all clank their beer bottles together and say, "Here, here."

Chief Tanner says, "Now that the whole Trynx 3 thing has been put to bed once and for all there will be memorials planned for those that lost their lives. The Planetary Police will have one for Carter and the EDF will have one for the special forces teams and the crews of the two cruisers we lost."

Nathan raises his beer and says, "To Carter."

They all clank their beer bottles together and say, "To Carter."

Mr. Black raises his beer and says, "To the special forces teams and to the crews on those cruisers."

They all clank their beer bottles together and say, "Here, here."

Chief Tanner raises his beer and says, "To the best damn team on the Planetary Police Force. Great job, everyone."

Once again, they all clank their beer bottles together and say, "Here, here."

Nathan starts a fire in the fire pit on the deck and everyone gathers around it to enjoy a few more drinks and talk about how great it feels knowing the time travel threat is no longer hanging over their heads.

Nathan doesn't say anything, but in the back of his mind he wonders if the threat has truly been eliminated. The Xandurians know time travel is possible, will they continue on their quest to go back in time and wipe Earth out so they can be the most powerful force in the galaxy? Will they develop another time machine and try to find an alternate power source for it? They will just have to wait and see what the future holds.

**THE END**

## EPILOGUE

The crews on the ships that remained at Trynx 3 are busy dismantling the web of satellites. It takes them a full week to retrieve all the satellites and store them back aboard the military freighter that originally brought them to Trynx 3. When the last satellite is secured in the hold, and all the small worker craft have returned to their ships, the ships set course back home to Earth and jump into FTL.

Ten seconds after the EDF fleet jumps, a lone Xandurian ship drops out of FTL and comes to a dead stop where Trynx 3 used to be. It sits motionless in space for a few moments and then begins to move again. It turns, flying a large sweeping arc around the area. When it has turned one hundred and eighty degrees, it accelerates away quickly and disappears in a bright blue flash of light as it jumps into FTL.

## GLOSSARY

**FTL** – this is an acronym for "faster than light" and in this book refers to the fact that a ship is traveling faster than the speed of light and also to the engines / drive that propels a ship to speeds faster than the speed of light.

**TSL** – this is an acronym for "times the speed of light" and in this book is a reference to the speed a ship is traveling at. In several instances in this book you will see a ship's speed referred to as 14 TSL which is the top speed achieved by the latest and greatest FTL drive so far. It reads as 14 times the speed of light, but that is not quite accurate. The actual speed is $14^3$ X the speed of light or 14 X 14 X 14 X the speed of light.

**RCS** – this is an acronym for "reaction control system" which is a spacecraft system that uses thrusters to provide attitude control, acceleration and braking.

## DID YOU ENJOY THIS STORY?

If you answered yes to the question above, I would appreciate it if you could spend a couple of minutes and leave a review on the book's page wherever you bought it. I am still a new author, this is only the second book I have published, and positive reviews of my book will help bring it to the attention of other readers.

You can see my other titles at: **seanpatrickposey.com**

## ABOUT THE AUTHOR

Sean Patrick Posey was born in Edmonton, Alberta, Canada in August of 1969 to parents Dave and Margaret Posey. Sean has two older brothers named Mark and Todd. Sean was hooked on science fiction at an early age. Some of his favorites include:

- Star Trek (TOS)
- Star Wars (original trilogy)
- Battlestar Galactica (TOS)
- Alien and Aliens
- Stargate Atlantis

Some of his other interests include classic 60s and 70s muscle cars, camping, fishing, martial arts, 3D computer animation and modeling, weight lifting and technology.

Sean graduated from the Northern Alberta Institute of Technology (NAIT) in 1992 earning his diploma in Computer Engineering Technology and has been an I.T. person for the last 27 years specializing in network design, installation and support.

Sean has two beautiful daughters from his first marriage named Alyssa and Sarah whom he loves dearly.

In January of 2017 he married the love of his life Nicole Hayman. Nicole is an American born in Los Angeles, but was living in St. Charles, Missouri when the couple met online. They spent 7 years in a long distance relationship before marrying and Nicole has now moved up to Edmonton to live with Sean.

Printed in Great Britain
by Amazon

39918329R00129